The One Who Knew

ELLA'S STORY

J. ELLE ROSS

J.E.RANCH PUBLISHING

The story, all names, characters, and incidents portrayed in this production are fictitious. No identification with actual persons (living or deceased), places, buildings, and products is intended or should be inferred.

Copyright © 2024 by J. Elle Ross

All rights reserved.

No part of this publication may be reproduced, distributed, or transmitted in any form or by any means, including photocopying, recording, or other electronic or mechanical methods, without the prior written permission of the publisher, except as permitted by U.S. copyright law. For permission requests, contact

JERanchPublishing@gmail.com or JElleRossBooks@gmail.com

ISBN (PRINT): 979-8-9914160-4-7 / ISBN (HARDBACK): 979-8-3056874-9-1 / ISBN (EBOOK): 979-8-9914160-3-0

LCCN: 2024921666

Printed in the United States

J.E.Ranch Publishing

First edition November 2024

Note to the Reader

Readers should be aware that this novel contains sensitive or difficult topics, especially for those who may have experienced similar trauma.

- Depictions of grief and loss

- Suggestions and scenes of child abuse and violence

- Sexual violence and abuse

- Graphic violence and death

A special message for those who have fought their way through their own trauma:

"The paradox of trauma is that it has both the power to destroy and the power to transform and resurrect."   -Peter Levine

CHAPTER ONE

Ella Delaney

SAN FRANCISCO

Today was turning out to be the best day ever for Ella Delaney. Not only was it her birthday—she was six years old now—but she also got to go shopping with Nanny Marge.

Ella had begged Mother and Father for a Cabbage Patch doll for weeks. None of her friends in her first-grade class had one yet, and she really, really wanted one. Finally, Mother said she could get it today since it was her birthday. She gave Nanny Marge cash and instructions to take Ella for the afternoon so that Mother could get ready in peace.

Another fun thing Ella would get to do today was go to one of her parents' fancy parties—she never got to go—and that meant she could finally wear one of her fancy dresses, one that flared out when she spun and spun really fast.

Now, as Ella stood in the doll aisle of the toy department, she studied each of her options carefully. These were very important decisions. Boy or girl? Definitely girl. No hair, straight hair, curly hair? Curly, because it's fun. Brown hair, blonde hair, red hair? Red, like her own.

After the choices were complete and the purchase was made, Ella tore open the package in the backseat of the car.

"What does her birth certificate say? What's her name?"

"You can read it. Try sounding it out," Nanny Marge encouraged as she buckled Ella in.

"Sam, sam-an, Samantha. Roo, Roo-bee, Ruby. Samantha Ruby!" Ella's eyes shone proud, waving the paper back and forth in the air with a delighted squeal.

"Good job. Oh hey, it's our song!" Nanny Marge turned the radio way up so they could sing their favorite song, *Girls Just Wanna Have Fun,* as loudly as they could, which always made Ella laugh so hard she could never finish singing it.

When they finally pulled into their driveway, Ella was so excited to show Mother and Father she opened the car door and almost jumped out before they were completely stopped.

"Miss Ella shut your door," Nanny Marge called out, shaking her head in amusement.

"Sorry!" She ran back to the car, Samantha Ruby clutched tightly in the crook of her arm, pushed the car door shut, then ran full force back to the house, charging through the front door.

Father was first in her line of sight. He was on the phone, the long coiling cord stretching from the wall to the dining table where he sat with a newspaper open.

"Don't *'Oh, Declan'* me, Tom. I'm telling you, it will be a circus out there. The Queen coming to San Francisco will get all of the IRA sympathizers out in droves. Protests, riots, who knows what ruckus they will cause back home."

Father was excited about something, and not in a good way. Father called it, 'getting his Irish up'. He would talk fast, and the music in his voice would get stronger. Mother was the same. It always made Ella a little sad that she didn't have what Nanny Marge called an accent like they did.

Ella's parents moved from Ireland to San Francisco a few years before she was born. Even though they made sure to move into an Irish-prominent neighborhood and joined some fancy Irish society club as soon as they could, Ella went to school here all her life, so she didn't have the pretty music in her voice.

Since Father's Irish was up, Ella steered clear of the dining room. Instead, she ran up the stairs to find Mother. As she reached the top of the staircase, Mother came out of her room, her strawberry blonde hair in giant curlers, a green mask caked on her face like some monster coming up from the swamp.

Ella giggled and thrust Samantha Ruby out to show her. "Mother, look!"

"Ella, stop this pounding about. You're making far too much noise. You'll give me a migraine, child. Where is Nanny Marge?

Marge? Marge!" Fiona called down from the top of the stair landing until Marge appeared.

"Yes, Mrs. Delaney?" she answered, looking up from the first floor.

"I need you to look for my grandmother's amethyst locket. I can't find it anywhere. And, please, start getting Ella ready. Quietly." She turned and started to stomp back into the bedroom.

Ella hung her head, all of the excitement evaporating from her. Without even trying, Ella could see it, lying in the rose bed. Now she would have to tell Mother where her locket was.

Ella hated telling Mother these things. She'd always look at her as if she were weird or, worse, scary. Not that it wasn't scary, or at least it used to be.

Since Ella could remember, sometimes she would know something she shouldn't know, could picture it so clearly as if she was looking straight at it. Mostly she saw things that were lost. Like Father's keys—he lost them all the time—or her toys after Nanny Marge would clean up, Ella could *see* which bin something was in. Other times, she would know something right before it happened. Like something said on TV or the phone about to ring. But sometimes, she would get feelings about people. Mostly good things, but bad things too. That was when it got scary.

Her parents never seemed too concerned about it. They never asked her about it, never took her to any doctors for it or anything like that. Sometimes they'd act weird around her, like something was wrong with her. But mostly, they ignored it, ignored her.

Nanny Marge never made Ella feel bad about her special power. She was the one who helped Ella try and make sense of it, especially when it scared her.

"When you see something bad or scary, pause for a moment. Remember that most of us are good and *bad inside. We conceal the parts we don't want to show. People don't think they have to hide their thoughts, so just because someone might think bad things doesn't always mean they'll act on them. You can't live your life that way, Miss Ella, in fear of the possibility of the bad. You have to live in spite of it."*

She even helped Ella try to practice, but Ella still couldn't control it. She would either know right away or not at all.

Barely audible, Ella mumbled, "It's in your garden, Mother, by the yellow roses. It fell off when you went out to cut some for the table last week."

Mother looked at her for a long time, giving her the look she had given her many times before—eyes full of disbelief and a bit of fear. She nodded once to Ella, then closed the door firmly behind her.

Defeated, Ella's shoulder slumped, Samantha Ruby forgotten, hanging by a hand and dragging on the floor.

"Miss Ella, come on down here. I have a surprise for you." Even though Nanny Marge tried to hide it from her, frustration was etched in the lines of her face.

Ella dragged her feet down the stairs, her nose scrunched up, determined not to cry. Crying was for babies, like five-year-olds.

"Come on, now," Nanny Marge beckoned.

When Ella finally reached the bottom of the stairs, Nanny Marge led her through the swinging doors into the kitchen. "Close your eyes, now. Nice and tight. No peeking."

Ella could hear her rummaging through the kitchen. The sound of the refrigerator door opening and closing, a match striking, then the smell of sulfur filling the air. Finally, she said, "Open your eyes."

A beautifully pink cupcake sat on the counter in front of her, a purple candle lit in the middle of all that frosting. Mother forgotten, Ella jumped up and down, clapping her hands.

Nanny Marge gave her a warning look, putting a finger to her lips, then smiled and winked as she quietly sang Happy Birthday.

Ella closed her eyes tight, made the biggest wish, and blew out the candle.

***

The minute they walked in, Ella was entranced. It was like a castle in a fairytale. The room was dim, light cast from candles flickering in silver candlesticks reflected off chandeliers with hundreds of hanging crystals that sparkled like diamonds. A band was set up in the corner of the large room, playing some upbeat Irish folk music. Men and women in black uniforms circulated throughout the room with fancy-looking trays filled with fancy-looking food.

Mother took Ella's coat, handing it to one of the black uniform people. "Even though it is family night, that doesn't mean children will be running wild. You will mind your manners first and foremost. Stay quiet, no shouting, no running about, and do not, by any means, go into rooms you are not permitted to go into."

"Fiona? That *is* you! Darling, I desperately need your help. You just can't get good service these days—such a disaster. The caterer is phenomenal, or at least she could be. She runs that little shop that does all those authentic Irish dishes. Well, she calls and says she can't do the party because she would have no one to watch her child. I'm giving her this chance to make a name for herself, and she wants to cancel for childcare issues? So, I had to tell her to bring the child. Such a hassle. And then the candlesticks..." The woman who rushed to them took Mother's arm and led her out of the room.

Ella stood with Samantha Ruby in one arm and Father standing on the other, looking unsure of what to do with her.

"You run along and find someone to play nicely with," he said, leading her further into the room.

Ella looked around but didn't see anyone close to her age. A small group of teenage girls were sneaking sips by the champagne fountain. Outside, a few boys were throwing a ball around to each other, but they were also older than she was.

"Declan, fine sir. Finally, a reasonable man," a voice boomed from a tall man as he approached them. "Tell these, otherwise gentlemen, about the woes of having a woman mayor of our great city."

With that, Father was gone.

Standing in the middle of a room full of adults in poofy dresses and heavily teased hair, Ella was alone.

Staying close to the walls so as not to bother anyone, she made her way from room to room, looking for somewhere to play with

Samantha Ruby. Soon, she discovered the food table and, next to that, the dessert table.

Looking around, making sure no one was watching her, Ella crept over to the desserts, her tummy already rumbling with anticipation.

"Hi."

Ella jumped at the unexpected voice. Across the desserts, a pair of big blue eyes looked at her through a tall cake arrangement.

Never one to be shy, Ella greeted the girl back with a boisterous, "hi!"

"I'm Erinne. My mom brought me. She made all these in her bakery. Want one?" Erinne, who looked about the same age as Ella, came around the table, her side ponytail bouncing with each step.

"Sure. I'm Ella, and this is Samantha Ruby." Ella held up the doll.

"This is Dream Date Barbie. She is in her party dress." Erinne smiled and held up a Barbie in a sparkling purple dress. "Ken has a party tux, too, but I couldn't find him."

Ella laughed. "That's because your dog Sadie ate his head. Your brother found him and didn't want you to be sad, so he hid him at the bottom of the trash bin." Ella could have smacked herself. She didn't want her new friend to look at her the way Mother did—like she was a freak. She hated when she forgot that other people couldn't see what she did, and that most of the time, it would scare them. But when she saw something so clearly, it was hard not to tell.

Erinne stared at Ella. "How do you know about Sadie? And my broth..."

"It's my birthday today! I'm six years old," Ella interrupted.

"Me too. It's not my birthday, but I'm six. I lost my front tooth." Erinne smiled a big, toothless grin to show the gap in front.

"Girls, have either of you eaten dinner yet? Save dessert until after." A pretty lady with dark hair and blue eyes like Erinne, wearing a black uniform and a white apron smudged with frosting, came out from the kitchen.

"But Mom, it's Ella's *birthday*," Erinne stated as if it were a fact her mother should have already known.

"Well, happy birthday Ella. And for that, you shall have a most special dessert. But for now, I'll make the two of you a plate of food first." The pretty lady led them back into the kitchen to a small table tucked in a breakfast nook. "Get on up there you two, your own special table."

Ella felt special indeed. It was her birthday, and she met a new girl who—she saw in her special way—would be her best friend, at least for as long as Ella lived. And they got to sit at a table all by themselves in the kitchen, where no one else was allowed. Laughing, both girls crawled onto the chairs, placing their dolls beside them.

Ella scanned Erinne's face, a slow smile spreading. "We will be best friends for the rest of my life."

Erinne looked at Ella curiously for a moment, smiled, and then shrugged. "Okay! I've always wanted a sister. I only have two older brothers. They smell weird and mostly ignore me."

For the rest of that evening, the two girls talked, giggled, and played as if they had always known each other.

CHAPTER TWO

Jeffrey Mason

ARKANSAS

Jeffrey Mason was collecting his uncle's beer cans to recycle for pennies again. His uncle never left him any money for groceries or anything else they might need in the god-forsaken trailer. At least he could make a few bucks with the damn cans.

He got creative finding ways to make some money, be it recycling or pawning some of the stuff he lifted from the rich dick-head kids at his school. They never noticed anything missing from their precious, privileged lives. He even sold those spoiled idiots some pot here and there. Whatever it took to eat.

His uncle worked most of the time, though there wasn't much to show for it. The lights stayed on and the trailer was their own, no one could kick them out on the streets, so at least that was something.

The rest of his uncle's hard-earned cash was drunk away, hence the small income Jeffrey made recycling.

Not that Jeffrey needed his uncle much anyway. He didn't need anyone. Not since Pop landed himself a life sentence for beating the shit out of his mother, almost killing her, along with all the other stupid shit he'd done. And not when his mother dumped him on her brother's doorstep at eight years old to go off who knew where. Jeffrey has basically been fending for himself ever since, especially now that he got his driver's license this past year. He was able to get himself wherever he needed to go to do whatever he wanted to do.

As luck would have it, while he was bagging the numerous cans left scattered around the trailer, he found one of his uncle's porn magazines. Dropping the bag, Jeffrey plopped down on the ratty couch, opened the magazine, and thumbed through the waxy pages. It was a good one, where the women were tied up in interesting positions, dressed in leather and chains. His arousal was almost immediate.

A quiet knock on the screen ripped him out of his fantasy.

"Go the fuck away."

"Jeffrey? It's me," the whisper of mousey Ingrid, who lived a few trailers down, drifted through the door.

Maybe it wasn't such a disturbance after all. Trying to get Ingrid to do all sorts of dirty things was a source of entertainment Jeffrey hadn't tired of yet.

He hid the magazine, straightened his pants to disguise his obvious excitement, and opened the door.

Ingrid quickly looked around the trailer park, making sure no one had seen her. Jeffrey knew she'd sneak out of the small window in her bathroom when she could, which was usually during their bizarre afternoon prayer ritual when her parents locked Ingrid and her siblings in their rooms for the hour. He'd asked her once why they did that, and she'd told him it was to contemplate their wickedness and ask for forgiveness for their sinful ways.

As far as he was concerned, Ingrid's parents were part of some religious cult, homeschooling all of their kids for fear the ways of the wicked world would ruin their precious spawn. That family was fucking loony tunes.

Jeffrey gave Ingrid a sideways smile and pulled her into the trailer, letting the screen slam behind her.

"Shh! They'll hear," Ingrid startled nervously.

"So what? What will they do, beat me?"

"They'll beat *me.*"

Jeffrey quieted her by crushing his mouth on hers, pushing his body against her, and letting her feel his hardness against her thigh.

She pretended to be shocked and tried to pull away, but Jeffrey held fast. "Uh-uh. Stay here. Feel this. You like it. This is why you keep coming back." He pulled her dress up and yanked her panties down, shoving his fingers against her, rubbing with a heat he could barely control.

"Jeffrey, I can't," Ingrid huffed, the breath sucked out of her. "It feels too good. I'll surely have to pray for hours for forgiveness."

"Shut. Up." Jeffrey inserted his fingers inside of her, rubbing her at the same time.

"Oh my god." Ingrid's body wracked with a violent shutter.

"My turn." Jeffrey turned Ingrid away from him, pressing her face against the wall.

"No. Jeffrey, I can't," Ingrid half protested, starting to move away from him. He pushed her up against the wall harder, holding her in place.

"Relax. I won't take your precious flower. Yet." But he wanted to. He might, anyway. A quick slip, and it would be done. She might be upset afterward, but she'd get over it. Then come back for more.

Maybe he would just put it in her ass. Yeah, maybe that would do for now. He held her against the wall, rubbed himself against the crack of her, rubbed hard, back and forth. He wasn't going to do it. He was just going to rub himself off on her, but at the last minute, when he was close to peaking, he grabbed himself and, with a quick thrust, shoved it inside of her ass.

"Stop! It hurts!" Ingrid cried, her tears and snot sliming the wall where he pressed her face.

When Ingrid screamed out, the explosion of pure bliss engulfed Jeffrey as he spilled his climax into her. Her cries only made his orgasm stronger, lasting longer than any time he had ever jerked himself off.

"It feels divine," Jeffrey moaned, his eyes rolling back in his head as he savored the pleasure of each stroke. When he was finished, he let Ingrid go.

She wiped her face, quickly pulled her half-torn panties back up, straightened her dress, and rushed to the door.

"Hey, it wasn't bad. You're still a virgin." Jeffrey fastened his pants, then went back and sat on the couch, watching as Ingrid straightened herself out. "And you got off too."

"I told you *no*. And that hurt," Ingrid sniffled as she walked out of the trailer, quietly closing the screen.

She'll be back for more. Jeffrey shrugged, pulling the magazine from the cushions where he had hidden it. It didn't take long to become aroused again.

CHAPTER THREE

Erinne Byrne

SAN FRANCISCO

rinne tried her hardest not to let her hands shake on the indicator as they waited for it to move across the Ouija board. It was bad enough that Ella had already teased her earlier for the hitch in her voice when she'd asked why they had to do this in the dark. Ella never answered. She only looked at her with a sneaky smile as she lit the candles she'd placed around the room, really setting the creepy atmosphere.

Ella's superpower, *The Knowing*—as they affectionately named it years before—has never weirded Erinne out. Not when Ella would know who was on the phone before it rang, or when she would know where something lost was, or how she would know what was hurt on a wounded animal they'd happen across. Which is why Ella swore she was going to become the best doctor, like, ever.

Never once did any of that scare Erinne. But *this* did.

"*Why* do we have to do this?"

"*Shh!* Concentrate."

Erinne quieted, peeking out of one eye. Ella was still as could be, eyes closed, breathing steadily in total concentration. Erinne closed her eyes again, gulping down the lump of fear stuck in her throat.

Then she heard it, a faint tapping, slowly getting louder. Nothing on the board moved, the indicator still painfully frozen. Still, the tapping got closer. Erinne's eyes popped open.

"Ella..."

"*Shh!*"

The door burst open behind them so hard that it rebounded off the wall behind it. Both Erinne and Ella jumped up screaming. Erinne's dog, Sadie, started barking in response.

"Sadie!" Erinne yelled as her heart hammered against her chest.

Both girls looked at each other and then started laughing hysterically.

"Jesus, you two. Why do you have to be so obnoxious?" Erick, the middle Byrne child, stomped down the hall from his room to Erinne's, slamming her door shut behind him, which made the girls laugh even harder.

"Oh, he's so funny when he's mad," Ella said, wiping laughing tears from her face.

"He acts all big and bad, but he's just a softie underneath all that pretending." Erinne got up and turned on the lights, petting the dog that almost gave her a heart attack.

"When do you think he'll tell your parents?" Ella asked, a woeful look passing over her face.

Last year, Ella told Erinne that Erick liked boys instead of girls. She'd said it made him anxious and sometimes confused, but what caused him pain was keeping it from their parents.

"Who knows? He still pretends to have crushes on girls that he never calls or goes out with," Erinne said, shrugging. "I don't know why he is so scared. It's the 90's. People aren't as mean as they used to be."

"Um, yeah, they are. Maybe even worse than before. But *your* parents are amazing. He needs them in his corner. Once he tells them, he'll feel so much better about everything. He'll be much more confident. Besides, Erick will eventually get his Happily Ever After."

Erinne looked back at Ella. Her voice had hushed and she had that far-away look on her face she got when *The Knowing* came to her.

"Well, that's good to know. I only want Erick to be happy. He deserves it," Erinne said, taking Ella's hand. Erinne smiled at her when the look faded away and was quickly replaced by embarrassment.

Ella's first reflex was always to try and hide *The Knowing*, to be ashamed of it. Her parents were the least understanding people Erinne had ever met. They made Ella think she was a freak when she had her moments of *Knowing*.

Erinne didn't care for Ella's parents. They made her so mad that she'd fantasized about putting them in their place on numerous occasions.

Like, when they were eight years old, Ella had woken up scream-ing from the nightmare she had a lot, the one about dying. Terrified, Ella went to her parent's bedroom, sure she was about to die. Instead of comforting her and reassuring her that everything was okay, her mother yelled at her for waking them, for talking nonsense, and for telling lies. After that, Ella never bothered her parents when she had those nightmares again. Between sobs, she'd told Erinne the next day. From that day on, Erinne couldn't stand Ella's parents.

Then again this year, on Ella's twelfth birthday, her parents said she was too old for Nanny Marge and told her they'd already let her go. They didn't even let Ella say goodbye. Nanny Marge had basically been Ella's mom in that house. Ella had come over to Erinne's house and cried and cried. Erinne's mom, Annabelle, felt so awful for Ella that she called Nanny Marge and had her come to their house so they could say their goodbyes.

Since then, Nanny Marge—just Marge now—and Annabelle be-came good friends and Ella got to see her all the time, so the joke was on Ella's parents.

"Anyway, my experiment failed," Ella sighed as she blew out all the candles.

"Okay, *now* will you tell me why we did this?" Erinne asked, reaching for the box to put the scary-as-hell Ouija board away. She fully intended to throw it in the trash as soon as possible. If she were brave enough, she'd burn it. But she'd seen too many horror movies and knew trying that was a very bad idea.

"I've never been able to control *The Knowing*. I thought if I opened myself up somehow, I'd finally be able to. Guess not."

"Bummer. Hey, maybe your powers will come full force when you go through puberty, like Teen Witch."

"I'm not a *witch*. I wish I was. Then I could do a lovespell on my parents, get them to like me. And then I would get all pretty and get the cute boy."

"Ella, you *are* pretty. Too pretty," Erinne scoffed and threw a pillow at Ella's head.

"Ow. Brat." Ella threw it back at her. "Besides, I have gone through puberty, thank you very much."

"What? When? Why didn't you tell me?" If Ella started her period and didn't tell Erinne, she would be *so* mad at her. They were supposed to be best friends, and best friends told each other *everything*. Besides, Erinne was eager to start hers, and she was older than Ella by four whole months.

"I'm telling you now. I started my period last night. My mom got so mad at me. I'm not even sure why. I never know why." The green of Ella's eyes brightened and teared up like they usually did when talking about her mother.

"E," Erinne scooted over to Ella and put her arms around her, "we can share my mom. She loves you as if you were one of us anyway."

"Okay. Can I move in, too?"

"Yes. We can share my room. Wouldn't that be the bomb? We would be like real sisters. You already have an "E" name and everything."

"Speaking of puberty, when my daughter has kids, I want them to call me G-ma, Gigi, or Gammy. Something fun, not boring, old Grandma."

Erinne shot a look at Ella. She swore that one day she'd get whiplash trying to keep up in their conversations. "You're twelve. You just got your *first* period. Why are you already thinking about grandkids? You're crazy." She nudged Ella.

"It's just something I wish I had time for."

"Oh my god, you're *not* going to die. You don't know everything, you know." The only time Erinne actually got angry with Ella was when she said that she was going to die young.

It was a knee-jerk reaction, shooting Ella down when she said that. Erinne definitely didn't want to be like Ella's parents, but it was the one thing that did scare her, besides Ouija boards. Erinne couldn't imagine losing her best friend, didn't even want to think about it because it hurt too much.

"Okay fine, enough of that. What is *our* fabulous mother making for dinner?"

CHAPTER FOUR

Jeffrey Mason

ARKANSAS

Life was not turning out how Jeffrey Mason had wanted or expected it to. At seventeen, he had been discarded and trapped all in one swoop. This time, he had only himself to blame, he supposed. His uncle had been all too eager to rid himself of the burden of Jeffrey once everyone found out that he had knocked up Ingrid.

Ingrid's parents had stormed their trailer, dragging along a sixteen-year-old, sniveling Ingrid, refusing to leave before confronting Jeffrey and his uncle. They demanded Jeffrey do right by their daughter and marry her before she gave birth to the bastard child since he had already damned her, and she would be forever denied life everlasting, doomed to burn in the fires of hell and all that crazy crap.

To Jeffrey's amazement, his uncle only laughed—at Jeffrey.

"You're some kind of dumb ass, kid."

He then signed permission for his minor nephew's marriage.

Jeffrey's first impulse was to take off to some far-off place without Ingrid, parents, or uncles. But he had zero money to go farther than the liquor store on the corner.

Instead, he accepted Ingrid's father's firm suggestion of taking a job at the factory where he worked, and married the plain, feeble Ingrid in a conference room at the county clerk's office.

He thought his luck was taking a turn when she miscarried. It could have had something to do with him knocking her around, might not have. But he was already stuck. It took money to get divorced, money he still didn't have.

Now, at twenty-two, he found a dull but consistent rhythm to his life. He would go to work—which he was actually pretty good at. So much so that after Ingrid's father died, the good ol' boys brought him into their group to be groomed and taught the ways of the older, wiser men.

In the evenings, he would go home, and on an adventurous night, he would test how far he could make Ingrid go. She'd occasionally let him do certain, more adventurous things to her. *Let him* might be a stretch, but she had been willing enough.

Darker urges had begun to take up larger residence in Jeffrey's mind, his fetishes amping up, the need to act them out intensifying. There was a line he couldn't cross with Ingrid unless he wanted his secret out of the bag. It wasn't long before Jeffrey had the first affair, or the second, and the third.

Fucking random women he had no obligation to helped keep those needs under control. Though, it was only a matter of time before it would get old, and his desires would grow to the point when he couldn't wrangle them in any longer.

Chapter Five

Ella

San Francisco

"This sucks so bad." Erinne couldn't stop crying.

"We will write to each other, and we can call every day," Ella sniffled, hugging Erinne close.

She was losing a piece of herself. This was worse than any breakup she ever had, and there had been a few. But those boys never had her heart like Erinne did. Erinne was her best friend, her sister, her soulmate.

But she had to act brave, if only for Erinne's sake.

Ella had been helping Erinne pack the last of her things in her room all afternoon. Her parents had already sold, thrown away, or packed up the rest of the house, but Erinne had been dragging her feet.

"The school year will be busy, but I can come visit you every summer."

Erinne wiped the tears that kept streaking down her cheeks. "You promise?"

Ella nodded.

"Even all the way from Stanford?"

"Cross my heart." Ella gestured an X across her chest.

"It's going to feel like I'm missing one of my limbs without you."

"You've definitely become my right-hand woman," Ella said and chuckled.

"This is so unfair. This summer was going to be the best one ever. We just graduated from high school, and you got accepted to Stanford. We are supposed to be celebrating." Erinne started crying again, wrapping Ella back in her arms.

"I know. But it's not like your grandparents intentionally got into that accident." Ella stroked Erinne's long, dark hair down her back.

"God, you're right. What an asshole I'm being." Erinne straightened up, wiped her face again, and blew her nose in the wad of tissues she was holding. "Okay. Okay. I'm pulling myself together now. Let's get these last boxes down to the truck."

For the next hour, the whole family finished loading up in silence. No one wanted to leave, but they had responsibilities to take care of.

The week before, they'd received a call from a hospital in Ireland notifying them that Erinne's grandparents had been in a serious automobile accident. Her grandfather hadn't made it, and they didn't think her grandmother would pull through, which she didn't.

Lantern Light Inn was the legacy of the Byrne family. It had been in their family for generations, and Erinne's grandparents had been running it for decades. With her grandparents gone, the doors had been closed for the first time since it had opened centuries before. It was an emotional choice, but ultimately, Erinne's parents decided to go home to Ireland to run Lantern Light.

Ella would have gone with them without hesitation. But Stanford, her dream college since she could remember, had just accepted her college application. She *had* to be a doctor so that she could use the *Knowing* for the greater good. And she would be good at it—no, one of the best. It was her calling. She knew it in her soul.

But at this moment, with every fiber of her being, Ella wanted to chuck the Stanford dream and crawl into the truck with the Byrne family. *Her* family, the family that mattered, the family that took her in and treated her like one of theirs, who loved her unconditionally the way her own family could not. Instead, she fought the urge and held firm.

"Ach. I'll miss you something fierce, Love." Annabelle said, kissing both cheeks and bringing Ella into a fierce hug.

"I'll miss you more than you know," Ella whispered back.

"Well, you'll come whenever you can, for as long as you can."

"I will."

"My turn. I am so proud of you, girl. Give 'em hell over there." Erinne's father, Brian Senior, took Ella into a bear hug, the kind that sent her into hysterical giggles when she was young, the kind that let her know she was loved and cared for. This was the father who actually raised her alongside Erinne, and Ella's heart was breaking piece by piece.

Ella nodded again, stifling the lump in her throat, holding back the sobs that wanted to tear out of her.

"Take it easy on those Ivy League boys. Have a little sympathy for their poor, preppy hearts." Brian Junior, Erinne's oldest brother, stepped over to her, ruffling her hair as he always did. As a girl of the '90s, this usually made her squeal and twist away before Brian could mess up the carefully over-teased and sprayed hair—which was his whole purpose. But now, it only made the loss of a brother that much harder.

Ella kissed Brian's cheek. "I will."

Then there was Erick, the sweetest heart of them all. He was already bawling when he hugged Ella. "Thank you. For being there for me when I wouldn't let anyone else in. You've always loved and supported me." Erick kissed Ella's cheek and held her close.

Ella lost it. The sobs she fought so hard to hold back won out, bursting from her as she and Erick held each other tight, rocking back and forth.

When she felt like she could form a sentence again, Ella pulled back from Erick. "Hey, don't be afraid when *the guy* wants to whisk you away." She winked and kissed Erick's cheek again.

The family piled into the truck, everyone but Erinne.

"This is it, then." Erinne shrugged and dropped her arms to her sides, her cheeks wet from the tears flowing down her face.

"This isn't *it*. This is only the beginning." Ella grabbed Erinne one last time, one last hug. "I love you. With all my heart. You are and always will be my soulmate."

"And you're mine."

Both girls stood in each other's arms, crying openly on the curb of the street. No one rushed them, no one made any remarks. The world stopped for their long goodbye.

***

"Lantern Light Inn," Erinne's voice carried through the thousands of miles of distance as though she were just in the next room.

"Hey there, stranger," Ella said, smiling into the phone. She called way too often, she knew. Even though they wrote letter after letter to each other, sometimes she just needed to hear Erinne's voice. Six months apart already felt like a lifetime.

"Ella, your phone bill is going to be astronomical."

"Meh, that's my parents' problem. They don't care as long as it keeps me out of their hair. Besides, I didn't want to wait to tell you my exciting news through a letter."

"Hold on, let me get Brian to man the front desk and go to my parent's office. One sec." Erinne put Ella on hold. Some fun Irish music played softly in the background.

"I'm back. Spill it."

"I'm moving into an apartment right off campus with two other students, Matt and Ruby. I have to get out of this house. It's like a freaking tomb." Ella looked around her bedroom. It was as it had always been. And yet, it was never hers. It had been whatever her mother's interior decorator made it. Her true room was Erinne's. She'd spent more time in that one than her own.

The first semester at Stanford was finished, and she was more than ready to move out, start her own adventures, and get out from under her parents' privileged superior thumbs. "I can't stand the coldness here. Since they've all but worn out their bragging rights about me going to Stanford, advancing themselves in their social circle as far as it's going to take them, they've barely spoken more than a few words to me."

"Yeah, well, screw them. But your own apartment? That's rad! You'll get, like, the real college experience. I'm kind of jealous."

"What are you talking about? You're about to get your own college experience. I'm so excited you took the plunge and signed up for business classes," Ella teased. It was always fun to slightly shock Erinne.

"Of course you know about that," Erinne chuckled on the other end.

"Of course I do. It's great, Erinne. Those business classes are going to be perfect for you. Lantern Light is going to be fantastic. You're going to transform it into this wonderful place. I know it."

"Because of your superpower."

"No, because I know *you*."

There was a pause in the line, then a hurried rush of words.

"Why do you have to stay there to become a fabulous doctor? Ireland is stunning. This peacefulness washed over me as soon as we got off the plane. And this place, Lantern Light, it's like it has a soul.

It's pretty small now, but people love coming here. Lantern Light could be a big destination spot. It's surrounded by woods on one side and cliffs on the other. You can see for miles out on the ocean. If you were here with me, we could make it into the greatest hotel in the world. Mom would do all the cooking, of course. I would do the design and our business plans. Dad and the brothers would do the build. Well, one brother, anyway. I have news, too, but we'll get back to that. You could be the guest relations guru because you can charm a snake, and everyone loves you. It would be perfect."

"It will be all of that and more, I promise you. What's your news?" Ella fluffed up her pillows and laid back on her bed, looking at the picture on the nightstand of her and Erinne taken when they were ten.

She wanted to run off to Ireland almost as badly as she wanted that medical degree. It was harder and harder not to every time she spoke to Erinne. The only thing holding her back in San Francisco was knowing she was *supposed* to be there. She wasn't sure why so much as felt it deep inside.

Ella never did figure out a way to control *The Knowing*, no matter how many crazy experiments she tried since she was a kid. When she saw something, had that picture so clear in her mind, or felt it deep within, she knew it was inevitable to try and fight it. No matter what she did to change it, the circumstances might alter, but the same outcome would come to fruition.

Besides, how could she abandon the ability to come up to someone sick or hurt and just *know* what was wrong? With schooling, she'd finally learn how to fix the hurt and heal the sick. She may have never learned to control her abilities, but she was learning how to hone them into a specialty. It was the least she could do with this superpower that had been more of a burden than a blessing.

She had long since stopped telling Erinne about the heavier stuff. As tough as Erinne was—the first one to stand up to bullies and the first to fight, always the protector—when Ella told her the harder things, Erinne would shut down and deny its existence, especially Ella's doomed timeline. She wasn't about to tell Erinne that the feeling was getting stronger by the month. Ella was only eighteen years old and could already hear the clock start the countdown to her end. The ticks were soft, but they were there.

"My news is about Erick. He met a dashing Englishman. His name is Rich, and the guy is hot. Whew. And that accent? My god, I almost wish he were straight so that I could steal him from Erick. Anyway, Rich is already trying to tempt him into moving away to London."

"Erick bagged himself an Englishman straight out the gate. That's awesome. When he moves to London, I am totally going with you to visit."

"Won't that be fun? Speaking of love. Are you still seeing Mr. Bartender?"

"Johnny? Nope. He ruined it by falling too much in love."

"Geez, Ella. Are you ever going to give any of them a chance? Poor guys. I wish I could be there to watch all the drama unfold. It would be like watching The Real World in person. You wait, one day, one of them is going to get into that heart of yours, and it's going to knock you on your ass. And I am going to love every second of it," Erinne challenged.

"I've loved them all in my own way. Love is anything you want it to be. Life is too short, especially mine. So, I want to fall in and out of love whenever I can. I want to live each moment. Truly taste things and savor them. I want to feel each feeling without holding back because tomorrow is never promised. You should try it, it's life changing."

"Shoot. With how often you're falling in and out of love, there won't be any men left for me. Even way over here. One sec," Erinne paused. Annabelle's voice was muffled in the background. "E, I gotta go. We'll talk soon?"

"Absolutely. I'll call you with the phone number of the new apartment when I get it."

"Love you. I miss you like a missing limb."

"An arm."

"Worse, a leg."

Chapter Six

Ella

Stanford

College was probably the best time of Ella's life, except for Erinne being thousands of miles away, which was the worst. Other than that, Ella was having fun.

She was surrounded by like-minded people in her classes and had more friends (except her best friend) than she ever thought possible. Best of all, she was free from her parent's disapproving stare.

Here, the boys were men, they were beautiful, and she had her pick of them. She tried each of them on, like new sweaters, just to see how they fit.

Parties were abundant, not that Ella went too crazy at them. She loved the music, the dancing, the laughing. Ruby, one of her roommates, had talked her into going to a homecoming baseball game and then to the celebratory after-party.

Ruby begged to go, stating that the whole team would be there, specifically the center-fielder Ruby had been crushing on the whole semester. So Ella went. Who was she to stop a budding love story?

Most of the team and half of the school were there celebrating their victory by the time they arrived. The music was loud, thumping through her body. Strobe lights flashed throughout the house, and already, some were stumbling about.

Ella grabbed a couple of drinks for her and Ruby, then found a few mutual friends. As they were all talking, the skin on Ella's arms dimpled, and the little hairs on the back of her neck stood. The urge to look behind her toward the back door overwhelmed her. The moment she did, the most beautiful man she'd ever seen stepped through. He was greeted by people as he walked in, and then he looked up, straight into Ella's eyes.

Shivers vibrated through her. Her heart rate kicked up a couple of notches, heat simmering along her skin, something she'd never experienced before.

"Oh, this is gonna be good," she said out loud.

Ruby looked up and followed Ella's gaze. "Chris Owens, shortstop. Careful, Ella. He's got a reputation."

"That makes it even better." Ella never looked away from him. Neither did he. Then he gave her a dazzling smile, half sweet, half sly. She could sense him, the way his lips would taste, how those capable hands would feel on her.

"Hey," his hazel eyes gleamed as he reached his hand out to her.

"Hello." When Ella shook his hand, he didn't let go. Instead, he led her out to the dance floor, pulled her close, and began to sway.

The boy could move, his hips expertly sweeping side to side. Never once did either of them break the eye contact.

She lost track of how many songs they danced to, body to body. Fast-paced, slow-paced, it didn't matter. Neither of them wanted to lose touch with the other. No words were needed. It was their bodies that spoke.

She shouldn't want him this much, this soon. But she did. And who was she to stop a budding love story?

"Let's go somewhere," Ella breathed in his ear.

"I'll follow you anywhere."

Ella laughed. "You don't even know my name."

"You don't know mine, either."

"Actually, I do. You're Chris, the shortstop."

Chris placed his hand over his heart. "I'm honored that you know who I am."

"My roommate told me as you walked over."

"Damn. Now I'm a little crushed. I hoped maybe you were a fan."

"I am now."

"It's a start. Where are we going, Miss...?"

"Ella."

"Never has there been a more beautiful name spoken."

Ella rolled her eyes. "No need to lay it on thick now. I already said I was a fan. Give me a second. I need to let my roommate know."

Chris held Ella's hand as they walked to her parked car down at the far end of the street. The glow of the few streetlamps accentuated the sandy color of his hair and the muscles that rippled underneath his fitted T-shirt. By the time they reached the car, Ella was breathless.

Not from the distance but because of the need to put her hands on him. Just walking close to him teased every nerve throughout her entire body.

Unable to wait a moment longer, she turned to him, grabbed him by that wonderful shirt, and pulled his lips to hers, devouring his mouth. His hands wrapped up in her hair as he took the kiss deep. She let her hands explore his body as he did with hers. The ache for him was so intense she had a mind to push him into her backseat and take him then and there.

"I'm all for this, more than anything. But we're kind of still in the middle of the street here," Chris said, out of breath.

"I'm about to have you take me right here on the trunk of my car."

"Damn, girl. You're killing me." He took her mouth again, picking her up easily, wrapping her legs around his waist, carrying her over until she was backed onto the trunk.

She left her long legs wrapped around him, pulling his body into hers. Still, it wasn't close enough.

"Hold on. Hold on." Chris broke the kiss. "I need a breath."

Ella smiled at him. "What's the matter, can't keep up?"

"Beautiful Ella. I can keep up, I promise you. But I do have standards to keep. I like to woo, at least a little bit."

"You want to stop right *now* to woo me?" She couldn't help but laugh.

"Oh, I really don't want to stop. But I want you to respect me in the morning." That sly, sweet, dazzling smile was back, lighting up his entire face. "I do have more to offer than just hot, incredible sex."

"You can prove that after. Start wooing me in the morning. Right now, I need that hot, incredible sex." Ella pulled him back in. If they waited one more minute, her body might incinerate.

He didn't protest again.

Ella was always up for anything. Spontaneity was what she loved so much about life. Living moment to moment, seizing whatever came her way, living like nothing lasts because, for her, it wouldn't. Even so, this wasn't her usual way.

But the hunger for this man was like nothing and no one before. The only way to burn it out of her was to take him as soon as she could, wherever they were. Which happened to be on the back of her car at the end of a dark street.

It might have been the first time Chris and Ella made love, but it wasn't even close to the last. The moment they joined together, Ella knew she'd never again be with anyone else.

CHAPTER SEVEN

Erinne

IRELAND

E rinne dove for the phone on the other side of the front desk, knocking over her textbook along with her ferociously scribbled notes. "Lantern Light Inn."

"I'm in love!"

"Again? With Mr. Frat Boy?" Erinne stretched the phone cord to reach the textbook and notepad that now lay upended on the floor.

"No. Not him, silly. He's still wonderful and all, but I wasn't the one for him," Ella's voice, light and happy as always, came through exceptionally clear, though they were thousands of miles apart.

"Okay. Makes sense. Though you say you're not the one for any of them."

"I'm not going to be around for too long, so I don't want to break these poor, beautiful boy's hearts."

"Ella, please, you're not going to die young. It breaks *my* heart every single time you say that."

"Which is why I'd never let you marry me, either. But it's too late. I already love you totally and completely. You're my soulmate, my soul sister."

"Yeah. Yeah. Such a sweet talker. So, who is the new beautiful boy?"

"He is, indeed, beautiful. But funny, like, really funny. My face hurts from smiling and laughing so much when I spend time with him. And he has such a lust for life, such a fun sense of adventure. He comes up with these crazy, spontaneous escapades. He's amazing. If anyone would be *the one*, it would have been him. He is... special."

"Does Mr. Special have a name?"

"Chris. His name is Chris," Ella sighed dreamily. "You have to meet him the next time you come out to visit. Hell, I should just surprise him for once with an adventure of my own and take him to Ireland."

Erinne could hear the smile in Ella's voice as she spoke about this guy. Ella sounded totally in love. Again. Who knows, maybe something *was* different this time.

"Speaking of visiting, I'm throwing in some design courses in addition to my business classes this semester. I don't think I'll be able to come out this winter."

"Boo. But I am so excited you're doing it. Erinne, your overhaul of Lantern Light will be more than amazing. It will change everything."

"I haven't even finished classes yet. Don't get too ahead of me. You know I don't deal with pressure very well."

"Well, it will. But okay. And speaking of class, I gotta run. I love you, E."

"Love you more, E2."

Chapter Eight

Ella

San Francisco

All the way to bio-chem, Ella's mind was consumed with thoughts of Chris. His smile, the way he constantly made her laugh, the beautiful body that accompanied that gorgeous face, and the equally exquisite ways he was able to move that body. Ella and Chris had been enjoying each other's company, both in public and eagerly so in private.

He was easy to be with, fun to venture off with. His love for a well-lived life matched hers, which was a first. No one had ever been able to keep up with her before. He was special, indeed.

They had the family thing in common as well. Like her, Chris came from a family who valued reputation above all else. The fact that Stanford recruited Chris to play baseball added to his family's social standing. But, like Ella, he never let that hinder how he chose to live, never let his parents' constant disappointment hamper his outlook. In fact, it motivated him to make sure he experienced the fun in each day.

Chris had a reputation for being a hummingbird, flitting from girl to girl, always keeping things uncomplicated, which served Ella just fine. Though she totally and completely enjoyed each person she dated, she never promised them anything long-term. That would be unkind to these men, and she tried to be anything but unkind.

It had been light and fun for months. When they both had the time, they would venture off together, exploring their surroundings, and most often ended up exploring each other in those surroundings.

Her favorite adventure so far had been a surprise drive down the coast. No matter how much she begged, Chris wouldn't tell her where he was taking her. He wouldn't even give her a hint. They drove for a couple of hours south along the scenic Pacific Coast Highway when a giant field of daisies filling the entire hillside came into view.

"Oh my god, Chris, look!" Pointing, Ella couldn't help the girlish squeal that escaped her.

He just gave her that smile and kissed her hand. "You said your favorite flowers were daisies."

"They are. The happiest of all the flowers."

"Ta-da," he said, gesturing as he pulled the car into a scenic turnout. He opened the car door for her, led her over by the hand, then helped her climb over the fence and into the fields.

"Are we allowed to go in this way?" Ella asked.

Chris shrugged his shoulders. "Probably not."

Ella couldn't stop giggling as they walked hand in hand through acres of whites and yellows and purples. She ran her fingers delicately over the petals. Chris watched her, a pleased look on his face.

The man left her breathless. He never stopped surprising her, and that was a feat in itself. Just his presence constantly teased her, igniting an ever-present heat through her.

Surrounded by nothing but daisies, she turned to him, pulling him into her so she could get her lips on his and her hands on his body, which led to the two of them making love on a bed of daisies in the middle of that field.

More often than not, Ella was thinking about Chris. During classes when she should be totally focused on what the professors were saying, during labs, while she studied. He occupied space in her brain that was seriously distracting and dangerously tempting.

She caught herself wanting to spend more and more time with him, missing him when they were apart. Ella couldn't *actually* fall for someone. It was best for the other person that she didn't. That ticking of the countdown clock only got louder as time went on.

So, she tried backing off. But that didn't work, either. She couldn't help herself. She was an addict, and Chris was her drug.

That is, until the second line on the pregnancy test appeared, a deep, dark pink.

CHAPTER NINE

Chris Owens

STANFORD

Life kept him on his toes, which was always welcome in Chris's world. He was game for whatever came his way. If his parents hadn't been the uppity snobs they were, he probably would have leaned more on the level, cautious side. However, watching them do everything in such a meticulously planned way proved how boring living that way was. He made sure to be 100% opposite.

He met his football idol, Steve Young, just because he and a group of friends decided at the last minute to follow the player bus after a game. Was it a good idea? Hell no. They probably should have been arrested. But after a morning of tailgating at Candlestick and then celebrating a dominant victory, it seemed like a great idea.

If he hadn't ditched his cousin's debutante ball—he was supposed to be her dutiful escort—to sub-in last minute for a varsity baseball game as a JV player, then he wouldn't have been persuaded to join the varsity team, which his buddy promised would be a blast and filled with all the hot cheerleaders a guy could want. Which then turned into being drafted by Stanford, which led him to this moment, sitting alone in his room, contemplating his next move.

The phone stared at him, daring him to use it so that he could finally hear her voice, hear her tell him the reason why she disappeared on him.

Usually, Chris was quickly distracted and would lose interest in a girl after a few weeks, at most. Not that he was ever cruel when he broke up with someone. He made sure to never get close enough or do things that would give the wrong impression to the lady he was dating. When things were called off, usually by him, they would part ways, mutually satisfied with the result. For the most part.

But Ella couldn't be so easily cast aside.

Ella was this mythological creature. She was beautiful, smart as hell, and funny, with a far superior wit—even to his own, and he prided himself on his comical genius. Ella had this zest for life that most were too afraid to harness, living each moment to its fullest potential. She had big dreams and even bigger goals, and she never expected anything of him. She'd never promised herself to him, nor did she ask him to pledge himself to her, which was new for him.

More often than not, Chris thought about Ella, craved her. He'd had several months with her, and his infatuation only grew. So, when she suddenly stopped returning his calls, he didn't let it go as he usually would. He went looking for an explanation.

He had waited outside her classes, but she never came out of any of them. He went to the apartment she and a couple of other students rented together just off campus. Matt, one of her roommates, informed him that she had moved out a couple of weeks before.

Usually, he would have given up at that moment. Obviously, she was blowing him off. He'd been given the boot. But for some reason, this time, he needed to know *why*.

Knowing she was done with him only made him think about her more. His gut was twisted up, and his mind was distracted. None of which was like him at all. And he didn't like it.

Then Chris got angry. How dare she walk away without giving him a reason. He would never do that to anyone, even in the worst relationship. So he kept looking for an answer.

When he was able to find the address of Ella's parent's home, he drove straight over, hoping to find Ella there.

He stood in front of the massive oak door for he didn't know how long, trying to muster up enough courage to face Ella. It was absurd. But then, he'd always been on the receiving end of this conversation.

The woman who answered the door looked at Chris as though he were an enemy worthy of starting a nuclear war.

"Um, hello..."

"Young man, you are not welcome here. Now or ever. Leave this property before I have you arrested."

Then, the woman slammed the door in his face.

Chris stood there, stunned. He couldn't move his feet from that doorstep, and he couldn't move his eyes away from the wood of the door that was inches from his face.

He had no idea who the woman was, though he had a pretty good idea he had just encountered Ella's mother, he had no clue what he had possibly done to offend her so righteously, and he still had no idea where Ella had disappeared to or why.

Yet, Chris still couldn't let it go. Couldn't let *her* go.

It really started to piss him off when he realized he couldn't function in his life without Ella—talking to her, seeing her, being with her, tasting her lips. A couple of months had passed since she ditched him, yet he was still losing sleep thinking of her.

It got to the point that he became unfocused during practice. So much so that the coach took him aside and gave him a Come-to-Jesus talk—get it together, or get out.

No one had ever had this kind of hold on him before. He should be fine by now, not wondering where she was, what she was doing, or if she was with someone else. He shouldn't still want her so badly.

And then Chris realized it was because he had never been in love with anyone before, and he was deeply, totally, and completely in love with Ella.

Then he'd run into Ruby after one of his games. They'd made the typical small talk, a quick catch-up. But as they parted ways, she'd said, "By the way, congratulations."

It all clicked.

He spent days tracking down people who might know how to get a hold of Ella's best friend, Erinne, in Ireland. He could have kicked himself for not trying to get a hold of Erinne sooner and kicked himself harder for not realizing what had made Ella flee.

Now he was staring at the phone, about to make the call that would change the rest of his life as soon as he dialed. Crazy thing was, he was all for it. Which was wild.

CHAPTER TEN

Erinne

IRELAND

There was a knock on her suite door. Erinne put the book she was reading down and got up to answer it. When she opened the door, she could have fainted from the shock that rippled through her.

Ella was standing in her doorway.

She didn't have that vibrant smile that lit the room, wasn't standing with her usual tall confidence. Never had Erinne seen Ella look the way she did at that moment. Usually, there was an ever-present radiance that all but glowed from Ella at all times. However, in her doorway, Ella looked dark and broken.

"What's wrong? What happened?" Erinne took Ella into her arms. She should have been elated at the surprise, but it scared her to see Ella like this.

"I'm pregnant."

Erinne stood back, looked at Ella. "Okay."

The word sounded way more confident than she felt. But it would be *okay*. She led Ella into her room and closed the door.

"What do you need? A shower, a bath, a nap?" Erinne needed something to keep her busy while she considered what to say and do.

Ella just stood there, and then she started crying. It was the worst sound in the world, Ella weeping. So instead of doing anything, Erinne held Ella for as long as the sobs wracked her body, even as she hiccupped after the tears ran out. She held her until Ella was the one to pull away.

"I'd say I needed some of that beautiful Irish whiskey, but..." Then Ella laughed. Not the kind of pity laugh one would have at a bad joke, but a full, joyous laugh, which made Erinne join in right along with her.

"A baby?" Erinne's eyes misted.

"A baby." Ella shrugged, but in her eyes was a happiness that she couldn't help. "Crazy, right?"

"Boy or girl?"

"I'm barely pregnant."

"You *Know*."

"Yeah, I do. She's a girl." Ella's smile spread wide.

"Oh my god, a baby, Ella," Erinne said, smiling. They hugged again and cried again. "Okay, we need snacks, lots of snacks, and hot cocoa. Unless you want tea?"

"No way, hot cocoa."

"I'll be right back."

***

"So, where *is* Mr. Special? What did he say? Do we hate him? I'm completely prepared to be all solidarity-sister." The fireplace was restoked and fully ablaze behind Erinne. The snacks they devoured spread across the rug like litter along a highway.

"I let Chris off the hook." Ella shrugged, popping another grape in her mouth.

Erinne looked at Ella, waiting for her to go on. Ella only looked back at Erinne, not saying a word more.

"Okay. We'll come back to that. What about your parents, what did *they* do?"

"My parents," Ella scoffed. "They said exactly what you'd think they'd say. How disappointed they were, how their reputation would suffer, and the kicker, how they didn't want me in their lives anymore because it was too much for *them* to handle. So, I stole the family album—Mom never gave a shit about family anyway—and left." Ella fingered the amethyst locket her mother had passed down to her on her twentieth birthday a couple of weeks before, the family heirloom Ella had actually looked forward to finally getting.

"Fuck them. They've never been there for you. You'll stay here with us, your real family. We'll take care of you. Wait, what about school?"

"I'm taking a break for now."

"Then you're staying here. You'll have an Irish baby in Ireland. It'll be grand," Erinne said with an exaggerated accent that she didn't actually possess. She'd always wanted one, like her parents had, but she was raised in San Francisco and sounded very Californian, much to her dismay.

"I don't know what I'd do without you, without all of you."

"Then it's a good thing we will never have to find out."

***

As expected, Erinne's family took Ella in with open arms, giving her all their love and support, as well as the adjoining room to Erinne's.

Finally, after all the years they'd wished for it, Erinne and Ella became the sisters they'd always dreamed of being. A little late in the game, but still a cherished time.

There were mornings, afternoons, and sometimes evenings when Erinne would hear Ella retching in her bathroom. She'd wet some washcloths with cool water, hold Ella's hair back, and hand her the washcloths.

It took a few weeks for the morning sickness to curb. After it did, Ella took on that glow they said pregnant women got. She was more radiant than ever, and the excitement was starting to build as her little tummy started to poke out ever so slightly.

***

"You should tell him, E." Erinne scrutinized her best friend with watchful eyes as the two of them manned the front desk, Ella staring off again with that distant look on her face.

Ella had become strangely quiet, not at all like her. Though Ella would never admit it, Erinne knew she was heartbroken over leaving Chris. Ella got scared and ran.

So not like her.

"Tell who what?" Ella's attention snapped back as she wiped down the desk.

"It's been a couple of months. You won't talk about him, not even with me. Do you think I can't tell that you're heartbroken? This is part of my Best-Friend-Sister-Soulmate job, you know." Erinne put her hand on Ella's to stop its wiping, wiping, wiping.

Finally, Ella looked up at Erinne, all that hurt in those green eyes of hers that mirrored her entire soul.

"I don't want to burden him, change his life. It's not fair to him. I should have realized who he was. I always knew I'd have a daughter, but I forgot about the guy who would give me the daughter. That's *my* mistake."

"Ella, that makes no sense. Hold on," Erinne quieted when guests walked in. She quickly checked them in, gave them a key to their room, and then called Brian over to cover the desk so they could walk outside and talk uninterrupted.

Walking along the cliffs that overlooked the sea had become their safe haven, a place for their more serious life talks, which they had a lot more of these days.

"Don't get me wrong. I am ecstatic to finally have you here with me, being roomies and all. When you showed up at our door, I thought it was my dream coming true. But not like this. You're having a baby. Which is wonderful. You think it's wonderful, I think it's wonderful. My parents are over the moon. Your parents—well, forget them. But you're sad, and it's not because of your parents being jerks. It's because of Chris. Besides, what *is* fair to him is to know. He has the right, honey."

"How could I do that to him? He has this great life, unattached, free to frolic wherever, whenever, and with whoever he pleases. He has this amazing, adventurous spirit. I don't want to be the one to kill that in him. What, do I call him and say, hey, no more adventures for you, sir? By the way, I'll be outta here soon, soooo, you'll be doing this alone?"

"But it's totally fine for *you* to do this alone? And stop saying you're going to die. That is not okay."

Ella took Erinne's hand in hers. "I'm sorry. I know it hurts you when I tell you that. Besides, I won't be doing this alone. I have you." They walked silently for a while. But silence never lasted too long with Ella.

"You know, this little girl is going to love it here. This land will be a part of her very soul. But please push her out of her comfort zone when it's time. She'll get too comfortable and forget how to live life." Ella put a hand to her tiny belly.

"A child of yours, not live a crazy adventurous life? Impossible." Erinne and Ella laughed, talking about the baby and everything they both hoped and dreamed for her.

Their talks along the cliffs always ground them both, bringing calm and clarity. When they returned to Lantern Light, Brian rushed out the front door, frustrated, waving them in.

"Will you get back to the desk so that I can finish the projects I am *supposed* to be doing. Shit, Erinne, I'm not a damn secretary. Speaking of which, there is a call for you, Ella. He said he'd wait on hold as long as it took." Without further explanation, Brian stalked off toward the stable.

"Oh shit." Ella's face turned a shade Erinne had never seen on her. Ella didn't get scared, rarely got mad, and certainly didn't let a conversation intimidate her. "It's Chris."

"Okay, okay. This is a good thing. It's time, Ella. You can do this." Erinne led her up the porch stairs and into her parent's office, where she could take the call in private. "You got this. I'll be at the desk if you need me." Erinne closed the door softly behind her.

Chapter Eleven

Ella

Ireland

Ella had never been so nervous in all of her life, never experienced the accompanying churn of the stomach, the hard thumping of the heart, or the tingles that traveled all the way down to the fingertips.

It was astonishing, really, that she hadn't felt this way when she missed her period. Nor was she scared when the second line on the stick turned pink. She wasn't afraid when she told her parents she was pregnant or when they cast her out of their lives, telling her that she was no longer their daughter. She didn't feel this way when she dropped her classes, moved out of her apartment, or packed everything important to her into a few boxes and left for Ireland.

All of those feelings hit her now, and it was just a phone call. A phone call that would confirm how broken her heart was, and worse, would break his heart. She cared for Chris too much to hurt him that way. Slowly, she reached for the phone, the red light blinking, blinking.

"Chris?"

"Why didn't you tell me, El?"

"I..."

Chris's face flashed before her. He had never been sad or angry, but right now, he was both, and it was because of her.

She closed her eyes and saw him so clearly—the smile, the laugh. He was holding their baby girl's hand, teaching her how to walk, how to ride a bike, how to make Mommy laugh insanely, and eating gobs of ice cream with her.

"It was shitty of me. I got scared. I'm so sorry."

"Well, it's a start." Chris blew out a shaky breath. "I get it. It's a big scary thing, and you went into survival mode. But you should have told me."

"Chris, I don't know what I was thinking."

"You can make it up to me later. I'm just so happy to hear your damn voice. Let me in, Ella. Let me be there for you, with you. I'll go to you if I need to. I know Erinne and her family are *your* family, and I know that's what you need right now. I won't get in the way of that. I just want to be a part of it."

"You'd come here?"

"Hell yeah, I will. I'll be on a plane tomorrow."

"What about..."

"*Nothing* is as important. School is a joke. I'm not going to be playing baseball my whole life. I can find work there. My family, well, they're assholes, so who cares what they think. Tell me the word, and I'm there."

"Why, Chris? I'll hold you back and eventually break your heart. You should be having fun, going out with other people, going on all your crazy escapades."

"*Other* people? El, you've botched that up for me. I can't joke my way out of this. You and our child *are* the rest of my life. It is only you. You are my biggest adventure. And I'm not wasting any more time."

"Do you even have a passport?"

"Am I not the adventure king? Of course I have a passport."

Chapter Twelve

Ella

Ireland

The year went by like a flash of a picture taken. Chris had been welcomed without question. He and Ella shared the room that adjoined with Erinne's. As a joke, they'd come up with a funny knock instead of the age-old sock on the door, just in case.

Chris and Ella didn't waste another moment rediscovering one another, making up for the months lost. Ella's ever-changing form intrigued Chris even more than before, and they couldn't get enough of each other.

Erinne and Ella would spend slow afternoons watching Chris and Brian bond over construction projects, Brian Senior teaching them both how to do certain things and how to work specific tools. After a day of good, hard work, the two of them would hang out and have a beer.

Even after Brian met Shelly, he hung out with Chris most evenings, and Shelly became part of the ladies' crew, who watched the men, laughing and teasing them about their adoring bro-mance.

It was a peaceful time for Ella. She ignored the loud ticking of the countdown clock, pushing it away from her mind so that she could enjoy those small but ever-so-important moments of her life.

What had been plaguing her thoughts was what would happen after she was gone. Her baby girl would be her moon and stars, but when she was gone, as the everlasting ticking reminded her, what would happen to her child? Ella would never stop living each moment for what it could be, but that didn't keep her from knowing that her precious time was short and to plan accordingly.

The baby inside her had grown to what seemed to be its peak, stretching her skin as far as humanly possible. The alien feeling of a knee or an elbow moving across her abdomen was a magic compared to nothing else. She already loved her daughter more than she loved anything ever before.

Annabelle was always fussing over Ella, making sure she was eating enough, drinking enough, resting enough. It was sweet. Ella couldn't imagine her life without them.

Where would she have ended up? Would she still be in her cell of a bedroom in San Francisco, prisoner to her parent's bidding and disappointment? She was thankful she'd never know.

On a crisp mid-spring morning, Ella was down in the stable petting the gentle old horse, Gypsy—the black and white paint that belonged to the land of Lantern Light as much as any of its human occupants—when an odd cringe crept through her back and around her abdomen. The horse nestled Ella's hand, pushing more than usual, neighing nervously. A silent pop she felt rather than heard, wet between her legs. Gypsy moved her head again as if telling Ella to get back to the house, whinnying softly. She didn't need to be told twice by the horse.

On her way back up to Lantern Light, she was brought to a stop with a pain unlike any other she'd ever had in her life. It was like lightning striking, starting from her abdomen, gripping its electric claws around the rest of her body and squeezing it like a vice. She bent over, clutching her belly, taking sharp, shaky breaths as the pain crested. When it finally subsided, she started walking again.

Chris was suddenly at her side. Ella had no idea where he'd come from or how he'd gotten to her so quickly, but he was there, his strong arm around her, the other holding her hand, guiding her back.

The moment they walked in through the backdoor of the Inn, Annabelle was upon them, then Erinne, and then Brian. Everyone was running about, talking quickly, excited, and nervous. The hospital was a thirty-minute drive with good weather, but as it was in Ireland, the roads were wet, and the rain was coming down steadily.

Brian Senior pulled out the four-wheel-drive truck and packed Ella, Chris, and most of the Byrne crew in with them. The drive was uneventful, with the exception of a few pains that would have brought Ella to her knees had she been standing. Chris looked like he would cry or pass out each time she had one. Erinne sat on Ella's other side, holding her hand, softly talking her through each pain.

Not long after she was admitted to the hospital, Ella's pains came faster. Erinne never left her side, and Chris stayed on her other. Annabelle cheered her on, holding a leg back, counting excitedly when it was time. Both Brians stayed out in the hall.

The evening came in moments, moments that she would measure her life in. The peak of excitement as the time drew near—the encouragement, the nervousness, and the love in that room immeasurable. Ella pushed when she was told, bearing down with a strength she never imagined she possessed. Then, there was a moment of absolute silence when no one made a sound.

The sweetest cry pierced the room, and everyone exhaled with relief, then cried with happiness.

The nurses placed the baby on Ella's chest as they wiped her down, encouraging her to keep crying. Ella wrapped her arms around the slick little body of the most beautiful creature, her baby girl. Already green eyes were wailing angrily, whisps of red hair drying.

Finally, as they settled the baby under Ella's hospital gown, she quieted in her mother's arms.

The baby looked up. Their souls connected.

Ella fell into unconditional, immense, fierce love that instant. Her whole life was meant for this. To bring this child into the world, to love her, to protect her.

"Welcome to the world, little Sera," Ella whispered to her daughter.

Ella looked up at Chris, who had tears trickling down his face. She reached out, cradled his cheek with her hand, and brought her lips to his.

"She's perfect," Chris said, awestruck, putting his finger in Sera's little hand, her tiny fingers immediately grabbing hold. "Marry me, Ella. Let's be a family."

Ella smiled up at Chris. "We *are* a family," she said, kissing him softly.

Erinne stood back, giving them their first moments together. But Ella needed her there, too, because she was just as much a part of the family she'd created. She motioned for Erinne to come closer.

"Thank you. For all that you've done, for everything you are," she said, putting her forehead to Erinne's. There were no words that Ella could say that would explain how much she felt, the love in her heart was so profound.

But that was the beauty of their friendship. Erinne knew Ella better than any other person, maybe even better than Ella knew herself. Erinne knew exactly what she was trying to tell her.

CHAPTER THIRTEEN

Jeffrey Mason

ARKANSAS

Over the years, Ingrid grew more and more rigid. With each pregnancy, she went further back to her holier-than-thou religious bullshit. Her cult ways were ridiculous, obnoxious, even.

To Ingrid, sex became an abomination, the worst of sins. Sex was only meant for reproductive purposes, never for pleasure. As time went on, she stopped letting Jeffrey touch her unless it was explicitly to make children, and he had never gotten her pregnant on purpose.

He took her if he wanted, willing or not. She was his wife, after all. As he would tell her afterward, it was part of her wifely duties. Wasn't *that* in the bible, too? Let her ball herself up on the bed and cry herself to sleep. He didn't care. It usually amused him when she behaved that way.

He'd wondered so many times over the years why she stayed. For fun, he would push limits to see how far he could go before she'd finally have enough and leave him. Strangely, she never did.

Maybe it was because her mother surely would never allow her back into their home as a divorced woman, or perhaps Ingrid stayed because she had zero skills to support her and the kids. Ingrid had never loved him, just as she knew he never felt much of anything for her. So maybe she'd been just as stuck as he was.

Not only had Ingrid become more like her mother in her extremist religious views, but also in looks. Plain, unattractively skinny, her long stringy hair pulled tightly back, always quiet, as mousy as ever. It disgusted him that this was his wife.

No matter. He had tired of her almost entirely now that she was pregnant with their second child.

In all fairness, there *were* a few moments when he thought about really trying. He'd put in the effort and time at work and made his way up in the company, getting some of the credit and recognition he deserved.

Another rare moment was when his son was born. Jeffrey finally felt a connection to something other than himself. He looked at his wife with an inkling of gratitude. That gratitude drove him to at least try to keep his tastes private.

But that had only lasted so long. Ingrid being extremely pregnant with kid number two made Jeffrey antsy and uneasy. The urges started coming on stronger than before, maybe too strong for him to control much longer.

And there was this chick at work who was hot for him. She never came out and said as much, but the way she looked at him told him all he needed to know.

CHAPTER FOURTEEN

Ella

IRELAND

It was time, she hated to admit, to return to San Francisco to finish what she started. Ella had been afraid and had run from everything. But life had a way of coming full circle.

Ella's entire pregnancy along with the first year of Sera's life in Ireland had been such a blessing. The Byrne family had been everything to Ella. Her support, her heart, and her love. From them, she learned how to be a mom and a family. They were her role models to aspire to.

She'd never be able to repay them for everything they'd given to her. Especially Erinne, when Ella knew there would be so much more to ask of her. But she would keep that to herself until the time came.

Ella would be forever grateful for those peaceful, heart-fulfilling years and would treasure them until the end. But Ella's fate was to return to school and continue working toward her medical degree.

The Knowing had never stopped pulling at her, pacing like a caged tiger, back and forth, needing to be released, its usefulness wasting away in its cage.

Ella and Erinne walked along the cliffs as they had probably done a hundred times before. This time, they walked with heavy hearts as Chris was packing up the last of their things to leave this place and its people that had become their sanctuary.

"I get why you have to go back. Can't say that I'm excited for you to leave, though. I'm selfish like that."

"You're the least selfish person I know, Erinne. We've had some amazing times, you and I, and made some great stories along the way with all the trouble we've gotten into."

"And out of. No one can stay upset with you for long. Not even that cop in junior year." Erinne laughed, even though tears wet her eyes.

"Your dad always said we were thunder and lightning, so I got this to remind you. When you wear it, remember all the trouble we made and the great times we had making it. Don't forget any of it." Ella pulled out a box that contained a diamond lightning bolt necklace. She motioned for Erinne to turn so that she could put it on her.

"Did I ever tell you, you're my hero?" Ella sang to Erinne, mostly because she couldn't stand seeing her sad for a moment longer.

"Oh my god. Shut up, dork." Erinne playfully pushed Ella, then wiped the tears from her cheeks.

"You really are, though. You were always my best birthday present. Don't forget that either." Ella hugged Erinne as her own tears started to spill over. In the distance, Ella saw Chris waving to them.

"I guess it's that time again."

"On to the next chapter."

"You said it, sister."

Arm in arm, Ella and Erinne walked back toward the Inn, where life would pull them apart once again.

***

It was like high school all over again, standing on that street, weeping. This time was no different, maybe even worse.

The entire family had become so attached to Sera. They loved her like a grandchild, a niece, a child of their own, and Sera loved them all. Hearing her baby cry for them as she and Chris drove away tore her heart into two pieces.

"You okay over there?" Chris kept his eyes on the tiny winding road, but he knew her too well.

"No. I'm not," Ella huffed, wiping her nose with a tissue as she tried to soothe Sera's cries along with her own.

"It's only for a little while. Maybe we'll come back, and you could practice here," Chris said, taking Ella's hand.

"No. We'll never get to come back here." The moment, the pictures she saw in her head, hit her hard and fast. Flashes tore through her mind, each picture bringing actual physical pain.

Hands of a man—no face—just hands.

A dark cabin in the woods.

A screwdriver.

Blood dripping to the floor.

"This is wrong. We shouldn't leave. If we stay, you'll both be safe. We should go back. Go back!" Ella grabbed at the wheel to make Chris pull over.

"Whoa. Hold on." Chris pulled off the road as best he could without putting them in the ditch. "What's going on?"

"Something is wrong. This is wrong. We need to go back."

"Did something happen to Erinne or the family?" Chris looked at Ella, confused and worried.

He was trying so hard to understand the cryptic messages spewing from her. She was giving him nothing but gibberish, scaring both him and Sera. Sera's wails got louder the more frantic Ella's voice got.

She took a few breaths, trying to calm herself.

"No, everyone is fine. I'm sorry. I haven't had one of these in a while." In fact, she hadn't had any since coming to Ireland. None during her entire pregnancy, and none during the whole first year of Sera's life. But now that they left Lantern Light, Ella had been hit with one like a freight train. "It's like it is trying to warn me. But I don't know exactly what or why. This thing has always been annoyingly cryptic. Not to mention inconvenient."

"Well, who likes taking the easy way? There's no fun in that. At least after you're done with med school, you'll put your *Knowing* to use. How can that be a bad thing? And when have you ever run from a challenge?"

"I ran from you."

"Yeah, but not for long. Look at us now." Chris winked and kissed Ella's hand. "Besides, when we get back to San Francisco, we're going to get hitched."

"Not if you know what's best for you." She kissed his cheek, then settled back in, ignoring the loud ticking all the way back to the airport.

Chapter Fifteen

Ella

San Francisco

Ella's status at Stanford was reinstated with a few additional requirements she would have to complete along with a short academic probation. All of which she passed with no problem. Chris had found a job with a construction crew that he enjoyed, enabling him to use the skills Brian Senior had taught him at Lantern Light.

Classes were going well, life was going well, and when she looked at her daughter, who was already almost two years old, there was nothing but pure joy and love.

It often made her think of her own mother. Her mother must have felt this way when Ella was a baby. Right? That feeling might have gotten lost as she grew older and became more challenging, but when she was a baby? Didn't every mother feel this way?

It surprised Ella that she actually missed her parents. Or maybe what she was missing was what could have been, that relationship they were never able to build.

She wanted to think that her parents might want to meet their first and only grandchild. Sera would undoubtedly enjoy having grandparents, seeing how much she adored Erinne's parents. Maybe Sera would bring them the happiness they never found in Ella.

Chris's parents had shut out all possibilities of any sort of relationship. They'd told Chris they would never accept Sera, that they didn't need that kind of talk among their peers. Ella's parents might be the same. But maybe, just maybe, they would surprise her this once.

One night, after Chris was at work and her assignments were finished, Ella mustered up just enough courage to bundle Sera and make the short drive to her parents' house.

Ella sat in the car way longer than she should have, staring at the house from the street.

She'd grown up here, yet it was as cold and unfamiliar as any other house on the street. Sitting there, looking at the house that could have been anyone's, ignited a determination in Ella to make theirs a warm and inviting home for Sera to grow up in. It might not be big or fancy, but it would be full of love and laughter.

Ella blew out a long breath, got out of the car, and unbuckled Sera from the car seat. Then she stood next to the car, unmoving, until she saw a neighbor's curtain conspicuously open and shut again.

Great, the cops would be called on her if she didn't make a move. Either back in the car or move her ass up the walkway.

Finally, she was at the door. Now, to just ring the bell. Her fingers didn't move. Sera squirmed in her arms. Minutes crawled by before she finally pushed the bell, her stomach dropping with the sound.

After what seemed like an eternity, her mother opened the door.

She just stood there, staring—first at Ella, then at Sera. For one fleeting moment, Ella thought, this is it, she is going to fall in love with her granddaughter. But her face was stone, and nothing was in her eyes but disappointment.

Leaving the door slightly ajar, her mother walked away from her. Not one word, not one expression, not one motion. She just walked away.

Ella wasn't sure how long she stood there in shock. She didn't expect much from her parents, but she expected *something*.

A few seconds later, Ella's father appeared at the door. He barely looked up, and he didn't bother looking at Sera. He pulled out his checkbook, scribbled something on one of them, then handed it to Ella.

"This is a one-time payoff. I don't need Fiona upset like this again. It's just better if you don't come back." He closed the door.

Fiona. Not even 'your mother'.

That was it. Ella no longer had parents. Sera would never have grandparents.

"Mama, can we be hungry now?" Sera started happily talking, bringing Ella back to where they were still standing. As she hurried back to the car, Ella vowed to never return to this house again.

Once they were in the car, all buckled in, Ella looked at the check amount. Apparently, her father wore a heavy conscience after all, or maybe felt guilty for what had become of their situation, or for their lack of parental love and support, or for just not giving a shit.

The check amount was enough to pay for the rest of Stanford, enough for a little house for them to plant roots in, and even enough to start a savings account for Sera's college fund.

Plans started forming as she drove back home. There were only a couple of weeks remaining in the semester. As soon as it ended, they could start looking at houses.

And then Ella remembered Alameda Island, a cute little town tucked in between two giant cities.

Erinne's parents had taken them there on a day trip back in junior high. The drive to and from the hospital and school might be a bit far, but that would only be temporary. She would find her dream hospital closer to home after she graduated.

Ella *Knew* Alameda Island would be the perfect place, with a perfect house waiting just for them.

CHAPTER SIXTEEN

Jeffrey Mason

SAN FRANCISCO

The children were somewhat entertaining at times, brief episodes of momentary delight. However, those moments were becoming fewer and farther between.

His daughter was especially appealing. Only five years old and already a beauty. Jeffrey found himself looking at her for longer periods of time, wondering what kind of woman she would grow into.

Lately, more often than not, he wondered what it would be like to feel her. Thinking about his little daughter, picturing those things was troubling, even to him.

Usually, he found other ways to get off. There was a particular porn shop he frequented that, for a handsome fee—for content as well as discretion—carried a secret room in the back that carried legal/illegal fetish pornography. But it did little to curb his lusts as they persisted in growing more ravenous.

Until he discovered specific places to go that, for the right price, would fulfill darker appetites and even more audacious fetishes. Jeffrey spent a lot of time there and more money than he should have. Even there, there was a limit to how far money went. He found that out when he was escorted out by a team of bouncers who easily outweighed him by fifty pounds, with a broken rib, a broken nose, and blacklisted from the establishment.

Then he'd made the mistake of fucking that woman from work. Bad move, as it had almost cost him his job.

That affair ended up being worse than sex with his wife. He learned too late that Marlene Jacobs only wanted vanilla, boring-as-hell sex. When Jeffrey tried to do somewhat unorthodox lascivious acts with Marlene, she all but called rape.

His team of good ol' boys got him out of that bind in a rare moment of luck. They assured him it had happened to all of them at one point or another. However, because a lawsuit had been filed against the company, they had to show that they 'took care' of the problem somehow.

They promoted him and sent him to run the start-up in San Francisco.

That was three years ago. It had only been a matter of time before the battle within started losing out to the hunger, making it harder to ignore than ever before.

It was Ingrid's fault, really. She left him blue-balled pretty much constantly, especially now that she was pregnant with their third child, a miracle in itself.

He hadn't touched her in years. But that night, he'd been on a drinking binge. Surprisingly, he not only got it up but apparently shot a goalie. He barely remembered it at all. He'd been frustrated with her, with the kids, with his life.

But then, he pictured himself smashing Ingrid's face with his fists, fantasizing about yanking her hair back, forcing himself into her mouth and wherever else he felt like, thrusting as hard as he wanted. Let her gag, let her writhe. Let her cry out and scream. And that is what got him rock hard.

He did exactly what he pictured, finally releasing some of what had been building inside. A few weeks later, she announces that she's pregnant. Again.

And baby makes three. Three godforsaken traps that drown him in this life he was stuck in. Jeffrey needed to find something to occupy his time, his mind, anything that might satiate the yearning—especially watching Ingrid's belly swell with yet another kid.

He started camping alone, as the kids would be the wrong type of distraction. Muir Woods became a place where he could lose himself. On one of his weekend hiking expeditions, Jeffrey found the cabin.

It was far from any other cabin and far enough off popular trails to be secluded and private, yet a mere forty-minute drive from the city.

The cabin would be the perfect place where he'd be able to let go and do whatever he needed to do to satisfy his urges in this pit of life he'd created for himself. A place that would allow him to store and expand his unique collection of photographs, movies, and magazines without fear of discovery. Sure, it needed a fair amount of repairs, but Jeffrey was handy enough.

He searched public records and found the current owners of the cabin, after which he contacted said owners and successfully negotiated the sale of one small cabin deep in Muir Woods.

More and more of his free time was spent carefully restoring his beloved cabin. He painstakingly considered each detail, from replacing old windows and removing old paneling from the walls, to laying new flooring.

Because there was no electricity at the cabin, he had to use his larger tools at home and then haul the materials from his house to the cabin. A small price to pay for a place that quickly became his sanctuary where he could be unabashedly himself.

It was because of the special attention to these details that led him to his destiny, to *her*.

Jeffrey was working on restoring the door frames that weekend when a piece of wood he was cutting kicked back on the table saw, sending the meat of his palm into the blade.

"Fuck!" Jeffrey screamed out, pulling his bloodied hand from the blade, holding fast to the flesh that hung free, bone visible through the gapping gash.

He grabbed a shop towel, wrapped his hand tightly, and drove to the closest hospital.

The dizziness pulled at his consciousness as he swerved into the parking lot. The loss of blood and the adrenaline wearing off had Jeffrey stumbling through the slider doors of the emergency department.

Security jumped up when they saw the blood dripping down his arm, his shirt soaked with it where he clutched his hand, immediately escorting him through the locked doors.

Nurses surrounded him, leading him to the closest available gurney, and began working immediately. He started to blink in and out of consciousness. He was undressed, leads were placed on his chest, a probe was placed on his finger, an IV line was started, and pain medications were given.

The angel appeared at his bedside only minutes later, the most exquisite vision in white he had ever seen. For a moment, he thought maybe he had died, and she was there to take him to the afterlife. But there was too much pain to be dead.

"Good afternoon, Mr. Mason. I am Dr. Wilson, and this is our student doctor, Ella Delaney. Are you up to answering some questions while Ms. Delaney and I assess your injuries?"

Jeffrey hadn't noticed the tall, older man standing with her. He had only seen *her*, the woman from his fantasies. He couldn't tear his eyes away from the green eyes that smiled back at him, her smile sweet and genuine, her long red braid cascading over her shoulder.

He wanted to touch that hair, pull it free from its binding and let it fall freely around that perfect face, run his fingers through it, and...

"Mr. Mason?" she spoke, her voice as sweet as the rest of her. "Are you okay? Can you hear us?"

"I'm sorry, I'm a little light-headed. They gave me something..."

"Yes, you were given a pretty strong pain medication. Just focus on my voice and answer what you can, alright?" She moved closer to him, watching the male doctor as he carefully unwound the now blood-soaked gauze from his mangled hand.

It was hard to keep his attention answering the questions, he was too focused on how her lips moved as she asked them. He told them what happened as best he could. She would smile after an answer here and there. How badly he wanted to keep that smile on her face.

"Delaney, come closer. Do you see how the blade's serrated teeth grated this muscle? It will make stitches a bit trickier. I'll show you how to do a maneuver that helps in these types of situations. I'll go put the orders in. While we wait for the supplies, if you'd irrigate and debride the wound." The male doctor stood to leave.

Jeffrey was alone with her.

"Don't worry, Mr. Mason, Dr. Wilson is one of our best here," Ella said, preparing the side table with supplies to clean his wound, then sat on the stool next to his gurney.

When she took his hand, two very different things happened simultaneously.

A flash of heat surged through Jeffrey Mason. An erotic heat that aroused him instantly. Careful to keep that hidden, he shifted his hip so that the sheet covered him inconspicuously.

This is what falling in love at first sight was like. He thought it was some bullshit fairytale morons told themselves to put hope in their pitiful mundane lives. But it was fucking real. He felt it, the jolt between them when she took his hand. Instant love. Lust. Both. It didn't matter.

As he walked to his car several hours and stitches later, he knew in his very being that this was the woman he was supposed to have as his partner in life. He knew it the moment he saw her, and she knew it, too.

When they joined hands, there was a connection. He saw it on her face, a recognition.

He had spent many years being patient. He tolerated the wife he was forced to take, tolerated the two-going-on-three children he'd made with that woman, tolerated the fuck-heads at work in order to be successful and not the pathetic trailer trash he'd come from. And now he was being presented with his gift for all of it.

He drove himself home to sleep off the grogginess of the drugs and dream of the new journey he was about to embark on. He was grateful for the maiming, for it led him to her.

Ella Delaney.

He was also glad it was his left hand, as he was right-handed. The doctor told him he might have damaged some of the nerves in that hand, and full feeling might never return completely. But he still had full capabilities of his right hand, which he had planned a lengthy use of when he got home and fantasized about *her*. The long red hair draped over her pale breasts, tickling his chest as she rode him. He could picture it so clearly.

Even when he pulled into his driveway, his son's bike strewn haphazardly in the driveway though he scolded him constantly to put the damn thing away or he'd trash it, and his boring wife blasting some awful back-woods gospel about some coming rapture, it didn't break his mood.

When he found Ingrid coming out of the bedroom, a pile of folded laundry in her arms resting above her pregnant belly, he had worked himself up so completely about the future doctor Ella Delaney that he shoved Ingrid back into the room, laundry scattering to the floor, slamming the door behind him with his foot.

"Jeffrey. Stop it. What are you doing? Don't. The baby. It is unclean. Stop it!" For once, Ingrid tried to fight him off, intensifying his arousal.

He reached out and grabbed the back of her head with his right hand, pulling her to him and crushing his face into hers. She pushed him away again, but this time, he slapped her across the face, hard, not once, but twice, sending her down to her knees.

Then he was on her, pushing her down on the floor, straddling her as he pinned both of her arms above her head to the floor. She tried to squirm free, but he held fast with his knees flanking her ribs.

"Stop it—the baby. Stop, Jeffrey!"

He let go of her hands and hit her closed-fisted until she lay there, whimpering. Jeffrey stood over her, looking down at her for a moment. He took a pillow from the bed.

When he put the pillow over Ingrid's face, she became Ella for him.

His body shuddered with lust, he wanted to devour her instantly, but also wanted to take his time. He took, pulled, bit into, tasted until he couldn't wait any longer. The sound of her screaming in such pleasurable pain made him climax quickly.

He took the pillow from her face. It was only Ingrid again.

Any trace of pleasure shriveled up along with the rest of him. When he got up, he noticed the blood. With any luck, she'd lose the kid after all.

With his mind still lingering on sweet, sweet Ella, he locked the door to the bathroom behind him to shower.

CHAPTER SEVENTEEN

Ella

SAN FRANCISCO

I t was rare that Ella had much time away from her books, away from rotations at the hospital, away from school in general. Chris's adventurous spirit hadn't dimmed over the years. He'd patiently wait until he could steal moments with Ella, take her and Sera away on some escapade—if only for a weekend or even a night—whenever he possibly could.

That night was one of those rare occasions. They even had a sitter, which was almost unheard of.

"You deserve a fancy evening. I'm talking the dress, the hair, the makeup. All of it." Chris slid up behind her while she was studying for the umpteenth hour at the dining table.

"Mmm. That sounds nice, but I have to..."

Chris put a finger on Ella's mouth, replaced it with his lips, and kissed her sweetly. When Ella opened her eyes, Chris was holding up two tickets. Her smile widened as she read San Francisco Symphony on the headline for that coming weekend.

"Chris." After all these years, he still found ways to take her breath away.

"Just say yes," he whispered, his lips touching hers again.

"Yes."

Shopping for the dress hadn't only been fun, it was quick. Ella and Sera—six already, how time flew by—went to the fanciest store she could find that was closest to them.

Sera was even more excited than Ella by all the flowing, shimmering fabrics. Sera picked some interesting dresses for Ella to try on, but she happily obliged, trying on each one. The first two made Sera giggle and shake her head. While Ella was trying on a third dress, Sera must have found something that caught her eye. When Ella opened the curtain, Sera wasn't there waiting.

"Sera?" Ella called out.

"Hold on, Mommy," Sera answered from the other side of the store. She ran back, holding what looked like miles of sparkling red fabric. "This is the one, Mama!" She thrust the dress at Ella.

"Okay, this is the last one, and then we have to get serious about finding a nice dress."

As Ella slipped the dress over her head, she knew before she even looked in the mirror. It fit as if it had been made just for her, and Chris would love it. When she opened the curtain, Sera gasped.

"Mama, you are so beautiful." Sera clapped her hands and rushed to hug her.

Her words were so sincere they made Ella's eyes tear. "Good choice, Baby Girl."

"It told me it was just for you."

"The dress told you that?" Ella looked at Sera, the most honest of faces nodded back at her enthusiastically.

Sera was like *her*, she would have her own special *Knowing*.

Her heart tugged. After years of hating it, Ella had found a way to live with the *Knowing*, even when it terrified her. That burden wasn't something she'd wanted to pass on, never wanting her daughter to feel that kind of affliction.

But Sera had something Ella never had, a mother who would explain what it was and what was happening to her. Ella would help her cope with such an ability and maybe even help her learn to cherish it.

Unlike her own parents, Ella would never act weird around Sera. Above all, she would never make Sera feel like something was wrong with her.

Ella kissed the top of Sera's head. "How about some ice cream on the way home?"

Ella followed the now cheering Sera to the front register.

***

Ella hadn't put on makeup or done her hair in so long that it took twice as long as it should have to get just right. But when she walked into the living room where Chris and Sera waited, the extra effort was worth their reactions alone.

Sera jumped up and down in her footsie pajamas. Chris looked at her—no, into her—making her heart pound a little harder, a little quicker. He had pure love in his eyes, and that love was for her.

It made her eyes mist over, which she fanned away immediately so that her painstakingly applied makeup didn't run.

"El. Wow." Chris lifted his hand to his heart. "Breathtaking."

There had been few times in Ella's life when she'd been shy, but this man and the way he was looking at her had the edges of shyness flushing her cheeks.

"Thank you. You're looking quite dapper yourself." Chris's suit fit him well, accentuating his muscular arms and the width of his chest, Ella's favorite part of his body. That smile of his bright as ever and still cunning, always looking as though he was up to something.

She might have convinced herself that she was protecting him all these years by not officially committing to him, but it was inevitable. She'd been completely his since they first locked eyes at that party. Maybe even before that.

The beauty of the instruments and the sounds of the symphony were nothing short of magical. The music touched Ella's soul. At one point, she even saw Chris wipe an eye, which he adamantly denied later.

After the concert, Chris and Ella walked hand in hand back to the car. They passed a street musician playing on the lawn in front of the City Hall building, his voice crooning a love song as he strummed his guitar.

Flashing that sly smile, Chris led Ella over to the grass. She quickly kicked off her heels, giggling like a girl as she followed him. He took her into his arms and began moving to the music with her, singing along softly in her ear. There weren't many things Ella didn't know about Chris after all their years together, but she'd had no idea that Chris had such a wonderful singing voice.

They swayed slowly, their eyes never leaving each other's. The night was clear, no fog or clouds in sight. The moon was mostly full, shining a glow down upon them, the man she loved more than anything serenading her as he held her in his strong arms. The night couldn't be more perfect—until Chris kissed her and kneeled on one knee.

Usually, when Chris proposed to Ella every few months or so, he would say it in passing, half joking, that smile daring her to accept. But not this time. Chris never looked more serious, his eyes wet with tears, as he reached into his pocket and pulled out a little black box, opening it to the most delicate, beautiful ring she'd ever seen.

"El, you are the strongest woman I have ever met. Your love for life is not only amazing, it's inspirational. I never thought I would be the type to fall in love. But then there was you, and I fell head over heels. I knew my life would never be the same again. You challenge me. You lift me up. Then you added the cherry on top by giving me the most perfect little girl. I don't know what I did to be the man who gets to hold your hand and kiss your lips. I don't deserve you or the beautiful life we've made. But I swear to you that I will work every single day to make you proud and to make sure you are loved completely. Ella, would you honor me and make me the happiest man alive by being my wife?" He kissed her hand, then whispered, "Just say yes."

Makeup forgotten, Ella let her tears flow freely down her cheeks. "Yes."

There was no denying that she couldn't live without this man by her side. No matter what might come to her, she wouldn't let it hold them apart any longer.

"A thousand times, yes."

Chris slid the pretty ring onto her finger, kissed her hand again, and then stood, pulling her into a kiss that pulsed down to her toes.

Applause erupted around them. Ella laughed through her tears as she looked up. She'd forgotten that anyone else had existed.

"Finally," Chris whispered in her ear.

CHAPTER EIGHTEEN

Ella

SAN FRANCISCO

"Don't worry, Mr. Mason. Dr. Wilson is one of our best here," Ella said, preparing the side table with supplies to clean her patient's wound and then sat on the stool next to his gurney.

When she took his hand, two very different things happened simultaneously.

A flash of heat surged through Ella, followed by ice-cold dread. Never had *The Knowing* hit her so drastically, never had such complete darkness engulfed her. She had to fight the immediate urge to drop his mangled hand.

She gulped down the overwhelming fear that wanted her to run, far and fast, and forced herself to continue as if the blanket of evil wasn't suffocating her.

She focused on cleaning the wound, careful not to look him in the eye. Not only would she not be able to hide her emotions, she might run screaming from this bay in the emergency room if he made eye contact with her. She could already feel his cold stare—the dark yearning in it.

She'd felt the oppressive air weigh down on her the second she and Dr. Wilson entered the bay where this man waited. At first glance, he looked like any other unassuming, aging male in his late thirties. But this was no regular man. Malevolence all but radiated off of him. It took every ounce of will to keep her facial expression devoid of the emotional turmoil brewing within. Every passing moment that she had to maintain physical contact with him increased the bile that burned as it rose to her throat.

By the time Dr. Wilson returned, her hands were shaking with trepidation.

"Dr. Wilson, I'd like to ask the nurses to show me where the supplies are kept for this procedure. Half the battle is knowing where things are in emergencies."

"Absolutely. I'll get him numbed up while you find the rest of the supplies."

She almost ran. She used every bit of self-control not to run from the hospital, get into her car, and leave without ever coming back—which was totally absurd.

A supply closet substituted instead. Ella rushed in, putting her back against the closed door as she tried to catch her breath.

She couldn't ruin this chance at fulfilling her dream. What would she say when they asked why she had left so drastically?

Oh, that guy gave me the heebie-jeebies, so I ran home to hide?

Ella had been way off her game lately. Not long after their engagement, Ella's usual go-with-the-flow attitude vanished, replaced by way more anxiety than she'd ever had in her lifetime. She was unable to shake the strange and constant uneasiness. The smallest things had Ella overthinking and overanalyzing.

So not like her.

She was in her third year of medical school, which was finally hospital rotations. The ER was far from her favorite specialty, but she was already learning so much. Yet, darkness loomed, tainting what should be the most exciting days of her life.

It wouldn't be the last time a dark personality came through. It was why she was meant to be a doctor, *The Knowing* allowing her to sense someone, what was making them sick, how to make it better, and how to fix them. It was also why she preferred to work in pediatrics, where the soul was still pure and undamaged.

But everyone had to do their rotations in each discipline. It made for a well-rounded doctor. Or so they said.

She could do this. All she had to do was make it through. She could get through anything for her daughter.

Ella took breath after shaky breath, focusing her mind on her beautiful daughter until she was steadier and her trembling hands calmed.

Inhaling one last time, she straightened her posture and, holding her head high, opened the door and went back to finish her job like the professional she was.

***

Later, as Ella changed out of her scrubs and back into her street clothes in the doctor's lounge, she thought about the encounter she'd had earlier in the day.

The person she encountered was bad enough, but the resulting panic attack was one of the worst feelings she had ever experienced.

What was that?

She'd never in her life had a panic attack. It was more than annoying finding herself immersed in these weird episodes. Maybe it was overexposure, too many personalities all at once, all in pain, or in need of something from her.

That had to be it.

Ella really needed to find a way to calm *The Knowing* down to a tolerable level at work. She had failed so many times trying to control it over her lifetime, but there had to be some way to at least mellow it.

Finally, her mind drifted to other, happier thoughts. She was on her way home to her fiancé and her daughter, and it was spaghetti night, Sera's favorite.

It had been a long day, and she missed her little girl and her little girl's daddy. Thinking of the life they had built and the family they'd made had Ella smiling the rest of the way home.

CHAPTER NINETEEN

Chris

ALAMEDA ISLAND

There were moments when Chris would sit and stare at his daughter. She was his miracle. He meant nothing more when he'd told Ella he didn't deserve her or this life that had been so generously handed to him.

In his previous life, he had fantasized about fortune and fame. Once he played professionally on a major league team, all of his dreams would finally come true.

He had been the most foolish of idiots.

None of that would have brought a fraction of the true happiness that conversing with his chatterbug daughter did on a daily basis.

Never once had he regretted giving up baseball. He never even missed it. He felt more joy teaching Sera how to use a mitt and catch with it than he ever had bringing his team to any victory. Teaching her the things he knew made him feel not only useful, but like he was contributing something to this world.

His family, the one he had made with Ella, had become everything to him. His job wasn't fancy, but it brought him more pride than anything else he'd ever done. If only because he'd learned a skill and worked hard using it. Working with like-minded people with similar values was also something he enjoyed—values his parents never had.

They had no idea what it was to earn something with their own two hands. Nor had his parents instilled in him what unconditional love felt like, as their approval had been solely based on his accomplishments and how those accomplishments would benefit them.

So when they turned their self-centered noses up at becoming grandparents in what was their idea of less-than-ideal circumstances, Chris couldn't say he was shocked or even surprised. It didn't bother him, though. They'd never really been significant enough in his life to give him pause.

Their loss.

Chris had found real, true love with Ella that he'd never before had in his life. A love that was not only unconditional but all-encompassing. He felt the heat for his soon-to-be wife in every fiber of his being, even after more than seven years together. Lust for each other had never waned, and his love grew stronger each day, along with admiration and respect for the woman who had his heart, the mother of his child.

His wife. His child.

Never in his wildest dreams would he have thought he'd find his purpose as a devoted family man, that nothing else would ever make him as happy as being Ella's man and Sera's father.

It was one of those chilly San Francisco afternoons on the island. The fog lingered throughout most of the day, and the temperature never really warmed up much. Yet as he built a fort with Sera in the dining room, he craved an ice cream outing—a love he knew Sera shared.

"Hey, kiddo. You know what I'm feeling right now?"

Sera popped her head up from behind a sheet she was tying to a chair. "Ice cream?" she squealed, jumping up.

"Yep. Let's do it. Mommy won't be home for another hour, plenty of time to hide the evidence. C'mon, off on another adventure," Chris announced, grabbing his keys and their jackets, a cheering Sera following close behind.

Sera continued chattering on the entire drive to the ice cream parlor, a quality she definitely inherited from her mother. Theirs was a home that was rarely quiet. Chris wouldn't have it any other way.

Once they had their cones in hand, he led Sera back outside, armed with a plethora of napkins. Sera had inherited Ella's clumsiness as well.

His cell phone rang.

"Hey, beautiful," he answered.

"Hey, beautiful yourself. What is my man up to?"

"Oh, you know, spoiling our perfect daughter, as usual."

"More ice cream, Chris? It's freezing outside."

"Builds character. Besides, she's got a jacket on. No worries, Mommy," he teased, listening to Ella's laughter on the other end. A sound he would never tire of. "I also made my famous spaghetti sauce."

"My heart. Have I mentioned how much I love that my man spoils me and my daughter so wonderfully?"

"'Yes, but don't let that stop you from telling him again."

"I adore you," Ella whispered and sighed.

"Good, because I'm obsessed with you. Now get your butt home. It's spaghetti night." This announcement had Sera cheering, then repeatedly chanting *'Spaghetti!'* in the background. "Maybe even a little dessert after our little one goes to sleep."

"But you've already had your ice cream."

"Say the word, and I'll bring some home to eat off of you. Better yet, you can eat it off me."

Ella laughed again. "Sounds like a plan. Love you. Forever and always."

"Love you back. See you soon."

Chris got up from the bench and wiped ice cream smudges off Sera's face and hands.

"Mommy is on her way home. Are you ready to go?" He ruffled her hair, making her giggle as he took her by the hand and led her back toward the car.

"Hey, did you know that your nose is smarter than your brain? It has more scents."

"You're so silly, Daddy," Sera laughed, skipping over the cracks in the sidewalk. "Do you *have* to go to work tonight?"

"No. I can stay home, and you can do my hair and makeup. Make me look pretty for Mommy."

"Nooo. Makeup *is* for Mommy."

"Okay then, I can do your hair and makeup."

"Nooo. Last time you tried to do my hair, it took Mommy a really long time to fix it," Sera said and laughed again.

"Oh man, I guess I better go to work since I'm not good at doing girly things."

"You are good at doing things! You're really good at teaching me how to play baseball and how to ride bikes. I only fell two times. And then you were good at making my knee ouchie stop hurting right after. Your magic kisses are even better than Mommy's. And you tell the best stories. You do all the voices and everything. And you are a really good singer."

Chris stopped short and put his hand over his heart. His daughter's compliments brought love, so intense, so pure, to the surface. Nothing Chris could have ever done, not even if he would have won the World Series, would have brought on the pride his heart felt at that moment.

If nothing else, he'd gotten this right.

"Why, those are the sweetest things anybody has ever said to me. Makes me tear right up," he exaggerated, wiping fake tears away, though real tears did arise.

He reached down and pulled her into a hug. When the threat of actual tears passed, he kissed the top of her head and let her go to open the car door.

He waited as his little girl crawled into the car and tried her hardest to independently buckle the seatbelt, which she didn't quite have enough strength to buckle yet, but insisted on trying to do herself every time. After a few seconds, Chris laughed and leaned in to help her.

CHAPTER TWENTY

Jeffrey Mason

SAN FRANCISCO

With the children staying at the neighbor's house and his wife under antepartum observation at the hospital, Jeffrey was free, giving him extra time to do whatever he wanted. He showed up at his job, put in the hours, then went home to the cabin, where he continued all of the necessary renovations. Especially now that he had a new deadline looming.

Each day, he went to the hospital. Not the one where his wife was admitted, but the teaching hospital where he'd met the love of his life.

The day after his serendipitous accident, he took a bouquet of flowers to the emergency room, where he asked for the beautiful doctor, Ella Delaney. The nurse who had greeted him at the intake window was all smiles at the flowers, going on about how it was such a sweet gesture and whatnot. But she was sorry to say that the medical students wouldn't return until Tuesday. He gave the flowers to the nurse, telling her it was to thank all of them for taking such good care of him.

On Tuesday, he went back, parked, and waited for Ella's shift to end. He followed her home, parking a few houses down, far enough away to be hidden in the shadows, and watched. He watched her park in the driveway next to a blue sedan. He watched her get out of the car, white coat draped over one arm, book bag slung over the other. He watched as she made her way to the house. Before she reached the door, it was flung open.

The most perfect child, a little girl who was an almost identical copy of Ella, came out. The little girl ran up to Ella, hugging her fiercely, making Ella laugh and nearly drop all of her things.

Exhilaration jolted through Jeffrey. Destiny had brought them into his life. These two creatures had been made especially for him, the trophies for his hard work and dedication.

A young man followed the child out of the house. The guy put an arm around Ella's shoulders, kissing her temple, then led the two of them into the house.

Interesting.

A husband? Boyfriend? Brother? He'd need to find out.

For the next several hours, Jeffrey sat in his car and watched the house. Windows would light or darken as they moved through rooms, curtains were closed when dusk set in. He only left after the last light had been shut off, and the house remained dark for a long period of time. The blue car never left its spot on the driveway.

He did this daily for weeks, diagramming her every move until he knew every hour of her schedule. He even grew so bold as to look through Ella's trash. There are so many intimate things one could learn about a person just by looking at what they discard from their lives.

Nothing deterred him from watching Ella, learning her routine, learning everything he could about her. Even after his wife had been discharged to continue bedrest at home. Their son was more than capable of helping care for his mother, allowing Jeffrey to make excuses of working late and rarely went home.

His mind obsessed over Ella Delaney, consuming every thought. He even called off work a few times—which he'd never done before—to get to know his future wife and daughter all the better.

On the days Ella was at the hospital, the guy would stay with the child, taking her to and from school, playing in the front yard with her. Dangerous, if you asked Jeffrey. The guy should have a mind to keep such a child hidden from the world. There was true evil out there waiting to do horrible things to such beautiful things.

On the nights Ella was home, the guy left for some mediocre job. That would be Jeffrey's window when he would take possession of his new family. He'd have no problem slipping into the house after the guy left for one of his shifts.

It took a while, but finally, the cabin was ready for them. He was ready as well. The itch was getting more aggressive. But he calmed himself, as this couldn't be rushed. It needed to be perfect, each little detail. The beautifully intelligent medical student and her perfect daughter would soon be his, to own, to possess, to have whenever he chose. All of his research, patience, and dedication would be rewarded.

Jeffrey told Ingrid he would be gone for the entire week for a business convention in Las Vegas. Ingrid seemed relieved to be rid of him. It didn't bother him, as he felt the same way toward her. Her mother would be flying in to care for her and the children while he was away. He was free once again. For good this time.

He barely slept the night before and got up extra early, not bothering to say goodbye to his horrid wife. He gathered his bags quickly and quietly, only hesitating momentarily at the doors of his children's rooms.

There was an odd pang in his chest, a quick pull of regret and guilt, knowing he wouldn't be returning and would most likely never see them again, also knowing who he was leaving them to be raised by.

Maybe he would bring the kids as soon as he had Ella and the girl settled. Maybe.

The day dragged on slower than usual, it seemed, waiting to put his plan in motion. For some reason, as he sat hidden in the shadows, he realized he'd never planned out what he'd do with the guy. He would draw too much attention too quickly. That was going to be a bigger problem than he anticipated. Jeffrey would have to get rid of him.

He would wait until the lights went out in the house, make his way in, then, quick and quiet, slash the guy's throat. There was plenty of land around the cabin to get rid of a body. Or maybe he'd throw it out on the side of some obscure road. There were plenty of rough neighborhoods to choose from. It would look like a random act of violence. Either way, once he was rid of the guy, he could claim his family. It was an easy plan. Effortless.

The front door opened. The guy came out with the child far too early. Ella shouldn't be home for at least another hour. The girl clapped her hands and skipped to the blue sedan, happier than usual.

Jeffrey started his car, waiting to follow discreetly behind. He followed them through the streets of the small island community until they pulled into the parking lot of an ice cream parlor. He watched as the two of them went inside and came out a few minutes later with cones, the child eagerly licking the side as the guy led her to an outdoor bench.

He watched the two of them for a long time, the little girl giggling at whatever the guy said. The easy way between the two of them began to brew a jealous rage. His own kids wanted nothing to do with him and mostly kept to themselves.

Jeffrey's son had his face plastered in video games most of the time. His daughter, about the little girl's age, was too timid—like her stupid mother—to want to do much with him when he was home. She was too scared of Ingrid's harsh tongue, which found any reason to scold her.

Your dress is too small, temptation is sinful. No jumping, you'll show your sinful parts. Stop yelling, we only shout for the Lord.

It was easier to avoid the whole situation that was his home life.

With this new family, Ella and the child would be his world. He would be the one who made them laugh. He would be the one Ella would look at with that playful smile she had. This would be his second chance, the chance to do it right.

His envy grew to rage the longer he watched. Waiting patiently and not acting before it was time became difficult, until it became impossible. The minutes ticked by slower and slower.

This guy didn't deserve them. He was glorified childcare, that was all. Jeffrey could kill the bastard right then, take the child from him, and gleefully watch the life in his eyes fade away.

The guy flipped open his cell phone and began speaking. It had to be her. She must be on her way home.

It was a terrible idea to change the plan at the last minute. He should wait until they got back to the house and carry out the plan he had meticulously made. But the rage took over.

Jeffrey got out of his car and quickly strolled over.

It was now or never.

CHAPTER TWENTY-ONE

Ella

SAN FRANCISCO

Spring rarely brought warm temperatures to the island. It was a chilly evening, but Chris had taken Sera out for ice cream. Ella couldn't help but laugh at the shared addiction between father and daughter. It could be snowing outside, and the two of them would still be guzzling down ice cream.

Her daughter also inherited Chris's sense of adventure and was always a willing participant in any of her father's antics. The two of them were always conspiring to whisk Ella away from her books and the hours of grueling studying she was always doing. Most of the time, it was a welcome distraction.

Always mindful of Ella's precious little time, Chris kept their adventures short and sweet. She hoped that Sera would keep that adventurous spirit.

If she allowed herself to fantasize, Ella could definitely imagine a long and happy life with Chris. God knew he'd asked enough over the years.

Ella wasn't ashamed to admit that she loved the look and feel of the pretty ring on her finger. She never wore it to the hospital, afraid to lose it. Even though it had only been a few weeks since she had said yes, she already felt the absence of the ring when she didn't wear it.

As she came to a stop at a light on her way home, an abrupt, cold fear surged through her. Her entire body began to tremble as absolute doom pressed down on her. The moment the light turned green, she accelerated, driving as fast as she dared.

She had to get to them. She needed to get to her daughter.

When she swung into the driveway, Chris's car was in its usual spot, and he was still sitting inside.

Bizarre.

The feeling wouldn't subside as she quickly pulled into the open garage, her fingers shaking so badly she almost dropped the keys from the ignition. She looked in the rearview mirror.

Chris didn't get out of the car, his 49er cap tucked low, looking downward. He was probably just on his cell phone.

Still, the dread didn't ease.

She prayed that her wobbly legs would support her as she got out of the car and walked over. When she got to the open driver's side window, she saw her daughter sprawled across the front seat, asleep, her head on the lap of a man who was *not* Chris, a knife to her baby girl's throat.

"Don't even think about screaming, or she's dead."

Ella's body stopped quivering.

This was the moment she'd dreaded her entire life. This was how it would end for her.

Whatever happened to her, whatever she did, she refused to let it include her daughter's life.

She quietly went to the passenger side, got in, and softly closed the door. Finally, Ella saw the face under Chris's ball cap.

"You."

"You remember me. Of course, you would. You felt it, too, our connection. I knew you did." Jeffrey Mason started the car and slowly backed out of the driveway to avoid drawing attention to them.

Once they were safely past the toll road cameras of I-580, he took the knife away from Sera's throat and threw the cap onto the floorboard, his slightly overgrown, thinning hair slick across his moist forehead.

Ella gathered her daughter up, clutching her closely, willing her arms to keep Sera safe, no matter the cost.

"What did you give her?" Ella's voice growled low and dangerous.

"That is what I have grown to love most about you. Mama Bear, first and foremost. The intelligence is a welcome bonus. Don't get me wrong, your beauty can't be compared, but anyone can be beautiful. Most of those with beauty let it lead their lives. But not you. Don't worry, Mama Bear, it is just the smallest amount of chloroform. She should be waking up soon." Jeffrey reached over to stroke Sera's knee.

Ella yanked Sera away from his touch. "You will not touch my daughter. I will kill you first."

"I'd be very careful if I were you. You're not exactly in any position to negotiate terms. If you want to continue such a blessed life and you want Sera to continue her happy existence, you will listen carefully. There are rules, and you will follow them precisely. Little Sera here has some of your fire, so getting her to understand these rules might take some work. I'm getting ahead of myself. We will get into all that later. For now, you're going to take that cloth there and take a few nice deep breaths. I don't want you to ruin the surprise. I've worked really hard to make it worthy of my new family."

"I'd rather stay awake."

With a disappointed sigh, Jeffrey yanked the steering wheel hard right to the side of the road and slammed the brakes, sending debris and dirt flying. In one fluid movement, he reached over, grabbed a handful of Sera's hair, yanked her out of Ella's arms, putting the knife back to Sera's throat.

He had been fast, too fast. Faster than Ella expected. She wouldn't make the mistake of underestimating him again.

"No!" Ella grabbed for Sera, trying to pull her back. A bead of blood appeared as the knife pierced Sera's delicate skin and slowly rolled down her throat.

"See what you made me do?"

Ella let go. "Don't hurt my baby. Please."

"What did I just get finished telling you?" The knife cut deeper, another bead of blood.

"I'll follow your rules. I will, I promise. Please stop. You're cutting her," she whimpered as tears began to fall. The complete terror of not being able to protect her child broke her will of defiance. Sera's well-being was more important than anything else. Ella would do whatever he wanted as long as it kept Sera safe.

"Consequences of breaking the rules will not be pleasant. Not for me, either. I don't want to hurt you or little Sera. I love you both. But I will punish you. Is that clear?"

"Crystal."

Jeffrey pushed Sera back into Ella's arms, watching her, waiting for her to comply.

Ella kissed Sera's forehead, took the cloth from Jeffrey, and placed it over her mouth and nose, breathing in deeply until she was light-headed and drifted away.

CHAPTER TWENTY-TWO

Erinne

IRELAND

It was a rare sunny spring morning in Ireland, warm enough to open the windows and let fresh air circulate through the rooms as Erinne applied a fresh coat of paint in one of the suites, readying Lantern Light for the summer.

The birds sang their songs, the breeze whispered through the grass, and the ocean crashed in the distance.

Though it was still early spring, repairs needed to be made, orders filled, and rooms perfected before the tourist crowds started coming back.

Her cell phone rang.

Smiling, Erinne placed the roller in the tray to retrieve her phone from her back pocket, expecting it to finally be Ella calling with some wild story about where she had been the past couple of days.

They communicated, in some way, every day. A call, a letter, a Skype session on the computer. But too much time had passed, and Ella was still AWOL, which worried Erinne.

The only thing that stopped Erinne from calling Alameda Island's police department to do a wellness check was that once in a while, Chris could coax Ella away from her studies and take her and Sera on one of his adventures. Those trips were always short and sweet, as extra time was sparse, and Ella didn't have much time away from school or the hospital.

Ella would always tell Erinne when they'd be gone. Until this time, that is.

It had definitely been too long.

Erinne flipped open her cell phone and looked at the number calling. It was from the San Francisco area, but not a number she recognized. An ominous chill pierced her body as she answered.

Her worst nightmare had become real, something Erinne had never wanted to think about, even got angry at Ella every time she mentioned it over the decades. Though Ella had insisted this would eventually come, nothing could've prepared Erinne for the moment she received the worst news of her life.

Almost stumbling down the stairs, Erinne made her way into the kitchen, where her mother was prepping the next day's menus.

"They found Chris...Chris's body. He's gone. Oh god..." As soon as she saw her mother, Erinne couldn't hold back the sobs.

"What? What are you saying? Dear God." Annabelle caught Erinne in her arms, sinking with her to the cold kitchen floor, wrapping herself with her daughter, and wept with her.

When Brian walked into the kitchen and found them, he joined them, tears and all, when he heard the news of his friend's fate.

***

"We have a little room on the credit card to get you to San Francisco. I wish we could go with you," Annabelle said as she helped Erinne pack a suitcase so that she could catch her flight back to the States.

"You're doing enough. I'm sorry to leave you without help."

"Nonsense. God willing, those girls are okay. You go, be the beacon of light for our girls to find their way back home to."

"What if..." Erinne couldn't let herself finish the words that stuck in her throat. If she said them out loud, it might make it come true, and she didn't want to think about that possibility. Not yet.

"No. Don't think it. She is strong."

"Ella always said...Damn it." Erinne stopped folding, dropping to the bed, and crying again.

"Ella was wrong sometimes, too." Annabelle wiped the tears from her own face as she went to Erinne's side. She took her by the shoulders, forcing Erinne to look up at her. "Ella was wrong sometimes, too."

Erinne nodded, took a few deep breaths, and started packing again.

Ella *had* been wrong at times, but something in her heart told her that Ella wouldn't be so lucky to be wrong this time.

***

Erinne had been at Ella's house for two days, which meant the sun was now setting on the sixth day since Ella and Sera had gone missing. Police had conducted daily searches, complete with search dogs, but no one had found any trace of them.

The last hints of hope were fraying at the ends. However, she couldn't lose faith now. She had to hold on to any atom she could to get through. Erinne could still feel Ella, her best friend, her sister, soulmate. Ella couldn't be gone, she had to believe that.

Erinne wrapped herself in a blanket on the couch and turned on the news, hoping for any shred of information. As report after report drudged on with nothing new on Ella or Sera, Erinne turned the TV off. She couldn't stand all the evil in the world, and the news was full of it, one story after another, of the horrendous things people did to each other.

She'd make tea instead.

While waiting for the kettle to boil, a wave of cold grief blasted her.

"No. No. No. No."

Again, Erinne found herself on the kitchen floor. Her body trembled as she emptied a wail of the worst pain she had ever had in her life.

She cried for the little girl who had so easily befriended her, who she played Barbies with, laughed, and grew up with. For the teenager who she stumbled through boys, clothes, hair, and makeup with. For the woman who had been an inspiration, between conquering college and becoming a mother. For all of the laughter and tears they'd shed through a lifetime together. Erinne cried for the smile she would never see again.

Even after her tears stopped, Erinne stayed on the kitchen floor. She'd sat there so long that both legs were numb when she jumped up to get her phone when it rang.

She didn't want to answer it. It wouldn't be real if she didn't answer the call, it wouldn't be true. The phone stopped ringing. A few seconds later, the notification for a voicemail dinged. Then the phone started ringing again.

"Yes?" the single word croaked out.

"Erinne Byrne?" a deep official sounding voice asked.

"Yes."

"This is Officer Stan Walters. We found Sera. She's been taken to Merin General Hospital. You're her guardian, right? We'll need you to meet us there as soon as possible."

"Sera. She's...she's alive?" Erinne stuttered, the oddest sense of joy, relief, and utter grief twisting like a tornado in her gut, especially when she heard the word *"guardian."*

"She is. Can you be at the hospital within the hour?"

"Yes. Yes, I'll leave immediately."

She couldn't ask about Ella, Not yet. She had to focus on Sera and concentrate on doing the next thing, which was to get to her.

Sera was *alive*.

Erinne should call her mother to let her know, but she didn't want to delay getting to Sera for one second longer.

***

The parking lot was full of news vans and cop cars, red and blue lights swirling, illuminating the entire lot. Erinne's legs wouldn't move as fast as she wanted them to as she ran into the hospital emergency room entrance. Inside, several uniformed officers were waiting.

"I'm Erinne Byrne. I'm here for Sera Delaney."

One of the officers stepped forward, holding out his hand. "I'm Officer Walters. I spoke to you on the phone. Let's go over here to talk." He took her to the ER doors, stopping before going through. "We got a call from a family off Hwy 1. They found Sera in the road. She is scared, and she isn't talking."

Nodding, Erinne snipped, "Just take me to her." Erinne couldn't stop wringing her hands together. One over the other, again and again.

He led her through the ER doors and past several waiting would-be patients on chairs. The constant beeping, monitors alarming, an overhead operator announcing codes and other ur-gent-sounding events booming over the moans of dire-looking peo-ple on gurney after gurney put Erinne's nerves on overload. The odor of antiseptic mixed with god only knew what thickened the air with illness, the room's warmth dizzying.

Sera was back here, all alone, with all of these sick people. She had to get her out of there.

As they walked past a nurse's station, a nurse popped up from her seat to join them.

"I'm Julie. I'm the nurse who has been taking care of little Miss Sera. I'll take you to her. I want to update you before we go in.

Our forensic nurse has just brought her back from the evidence extraction procedure. She wanted to stay with Sera until you were able to get here. I also want to warn you that it might be shocking when you see Sera. She's been through a lot. She is quite traumatized and won't talk to any of us," the nurse said, stopping in front of the closed curtain. "I'll let the doctor know you're here so she can update you on everything that is going on with Sera." Then she slowly opened the curtain.

Another nurse was sitting next to Sera, holding her hand. When she saw Erinne, she nodded, then got up to give them privacy.

All of the oxygen left Erinne's lungs. She had to restrain herself from gasping out loud.

Sera was in a hospital gown, finger-sized bruises all over her arms and legs, one leg twisted, swollen, and terribly purple. Abrasions branded her wrists and ankles, old blood caked around the ligature marks, new bruises blossomed over her little face, fading yellow-green ones marked the skin underneath.

"Oh, baby." Erinne rushed over and sat on her bed, pulling Sera into her arms, rocking with her, holding her as close as she could.

The tears came from Erinne's soul, anguish so deep, anger so fierce that Erinne now knew why people were acquitted by temporary insanity. If the person who did this walked in at that moment, she would not hesitate to murder the bastard with her bare hands in front of everyone here, including the policemen who were still standing around.

"Miss Byrne?" A woman wearing a white coat popped her head through the curtain. "I'm Dr. Moore. Can I have a minute?"

Erinne kissed Sera's cheeks and forehead. "I'll be right back, okay?" Sera didn't respond. She didn't look up. She hadn't even put her arms around Erinne when she held her. Sera just sat there.

"First, I wanted to extend my deepest sympathy." The doctor then began explaining the extent of Sera's injuries, telling her that a nurse specializing in forensics had been called in to gather evidence and assess Sera's internal injuries.

Internal injuries.

Erinne's worst fears were confirmed in those words.

The next several minutes were filled with a laundry list of all of Sera's other physical injuries, including results of X-rays, CT scans, lab results, and possible surgery on the broken leg, after which Doctor Moore finally said, "I strongly recommend that she also work with therapists for her emotional needs."

Erinne stood empty in a hallway full of other people. Her mind went numb. She couldn't think, couldn't speak. The child needed an immense amount of medical and psychiatric care, and she was now *her* responsibility. Scheduling all of the appointments, ensuring that Sera got the care she needed, making sure it all got done, making all of the decisions. The weight of it all now rested on Erinne's shoulders.

She looked over at Officer Walters, who was still standing at the nurses' station. She'd never be ready, but Erinne needed to hear it said out loud. She walked over to the officer, looked him in the eyes, and asked, "Have you found Ella, Sera's mother?"

The officer hesitated, looking away.

"Please. I have to know."

"I'm sorry, she didn't survive."

If he'd punched her in the stomach, it would have felt the same.

Erinne nodded, swallowing the sob that wanted to erupt from her. "When...when can I have her back?"

"Her body will be held until the investigation is complete. Then someone from the coroner's office will contact you and ask what your wishes are." The officer awkwardly put his hand on Erinne's shoulder. "I'm sorry for your loss."

Erinne nodded again because she had no idea what else to do. She couldn't lose it now, not with Sera so close by. She needed to be at her strongest to help Sera get through the hell she'd just been through.

Erinne would do that for Ella.

Erinne would do whatever it took, however long it took, to help Ella's daughter heal, to recover.

Once upon a time, Erinne had promised her best friend that she would take care of her most precious gift, the child Erinne watched come into this world.

It would be a long, hard road, but Erinne wouldn't rest if that's what it took to make sure she kept her promise to her sister, the best person she had ever known.

Afterword & Acknowledgements

And now...*You Know.*

Ella and Chris's story needed to be told. I am so happy that you've chosen to take the journey with the characters I've fallen in love with. I hope you, too, have fallen in love with love and live each moment to its absolute fullest.

After all, tomorrow is never promised.

Live like Ella.

Have Courage like Sera.

And have Heart like Erinne.

Writing means using up a lot of time and attention. Away from partners, kids (even grown ones), jobs, etc. All for a need, a dream, that may never come to fruition. But that need is so strong to tell the story trapped in your mind that you can't do anything else until it is told.

So I have to thank my husband, first and foremost, for giving me the freedom to do what I must do, and for listening to me yammer on and on about it.

I also want to thank the developmental editor for pointing out everything that needed improvement and encouraging the story's development into a stronger, tighter piece.

And, of course, thank you to my friends and co-workers who let me force upon them these lumps of clay that were this story in the making, begging for honest opinions. I must say, nurses really are the most avid set of readers. In our line of work, a morbid sense of humor is a must and makes for the best kind of beta readers.

And thank you, Bonnie, most of all. For letting me bleed your ears, for all your unconditional support, for all your words and encouragement. Thank you for letting me be in your life and for being not only my best friend—but my sister, my soulmate.

About the Author

J. Elle Ross is a California native, still residing in Southern California with her husband, three dogs, 26 chickens (since last count), and two turkeys (until November, that is). The four children have become adults and are doing their own thing, these days.

She is a writer by day, NICU RN by night, and a wannabe homesteader in between.

When not working with the babies, writing the stories, or tending to the animals and garden, she is reading anything she can get her hands on, watching way too many movies, binging TV shows, finding joy in stories in each and every form.

Also by J. Elle Ross

- **Someone Who Knows (Book One)**

- **The One Who Knew (Book Two)**

- **Those Who Know (Cinematic Edition-Both Books in chronological order)**

www.ingramcontent.com/pod-product-compliance
Lightning Source LLC
Chambersburg PA
CBHW061547310726

48972CB00008B/2642